I0587974

LISTEN WITHIN

A NOVEL OF DISCOVERY AND FINDING TRUE SELF

....

VICTORIA WRIGHT

© Copyright 2021 by Victoria Wright

All rights reserved. No part of this book may be reproduced in any form without permission in writing from the author. Reviewers may quote brief passages in review.
Published August 2021

DISCLAIMER
No part of this publication may be reproduced or transmitted in any form or by any means, mechanical or electronic, including photocopying or recording, or by any information storage and retrieval system, or transmitted by email without permission in writing from the author. Neither the author nor the publisher assumes any responsibility for errors, omissions, or contrary interpretations of the subject matter herein. The characters in this book are entirely fictional. Any resemblance to actual persons living or dead is entirely coincidental. Any perceived slight of any individual or organization is purely unintentional.

TABLE OF CONTENTS

CHAPTER 1 — SHIT HITS THE FAN

Robert, the director of our department, opened the video meeting. His glasses perched on the end of his nose, as they always were, he cleared his throat and said in a rather tense voice, "Good morning, everyone. Thanks for moving your schedules to make today's discussion. I just came out of a meeting with our CEO and some difficult decisions had to be made.

"Due to the pandemic and the significant decline in our revenue, we will need to downsize by thirty percent across the board. Please know this decision does not come lightly, and we understand what kind of impact this will have on the employees who will be let go.

"Susan will host meetings with each team leader to discuss the process and timeline. I look to all of you to manage this in the best way possible. I thank you in advance for doing the work that it will take to make the right decisions."

When Robert finished, there was dead silence. Unfortunately, for my colleague, John, he did not have his microphone on mute, and so we all heard his shock expressed in a series of colorful expletives.

"Thanks, John, for sharing your thoughts with the group," Robert said. "We are all feeling the impact."

You could see the shock on everyone's faces, even though many tried to look down or had turned off their cameras to hide their emotions. Looking back, I didn't think it was such a surprise, since there had been plenty of rumors going around about the loss of business. Not to mention, every day, we could see our stock price fall.

Robert closed the meeting, asking us all to start thinking about who our essential employees were and who would be put on the list to be laid off.

I sat there and thought, *Holy shit, this cannot be happening.* My team was already freaking out because of the pandemic and the mandate to work from home, and now I was going to have to lay off five people?

My entire body started to tremble with nervousness, knowing I would have to have life-changing discussions with people who I considered friends. How were they going to find new jobs? No one was even hiring.

I got up from the makeshift desk at my dining room table and took a couple of deep breaths. Walking around to calm myself, I then heard a *ping* and went back to my computer.

"Shit." My meeting with Susan was in five minutes.

I walked over to the mirror to make sure I looked okay. Who was I kidding? I looked like I had been run over by a Mack truck.

I moved closer to the mirror, pushed my bangs away from my eyes, looked myself in the eye, and said, "Evie, pull yourself together. This is corporate America, and it is not personal. To save the company, we have to cut the fat and become a lean machine. Better them than me … right?"

Then I thought to myself, *Nice pep talk … not.*

The call with Susan went as bad as I had expected. If our lives hadn't changed enough, these people would be losing their jobs within the week. At least I didn't have to do this in person. Virtual did have its benefits.

I submitted my list to Susan by the end of the day. Then I put meetings on all of my team members' calendars so, if they talked to each other, they wouldn't think anything was up. Then I shut down my computer and called it a night.

Tonight was a beer and French fries kind of night. Luckily, I didn't have to go out or order in, as I still had some frozen from my last shopping trip. So, thirty minutes later, I was in front of my television, dipping fries in ketchup and swilling beer. My table manners had definitely declined since lockdown.

There was nothing on TV, so I decided to call it an early night and try to get a good night's sleep. It had been a long, stressful day, yet I was, thankfully, able to fall right to sleep, as I always did with a couple of beers in me. Nevertheless, my sleep was anything but restful. My dreams were crazy and unrecognizable. I would wake with a start, fall back to sleep, and then have another wacked-out dream. I was cold then hot. I tossed and turned. My body felt like it was a wet shirt thumping around in the dryer.

Morning could not come soon enough.

***

When my alarm went off at six thirty a.m., I didn't feel like I had gotten any sleep at all. My body was sore and felt like someone had beat me. It was a two-cuppa morning just so I could get into the shower. Luckily, I didn't have many meetings.

By the end of the day, Susan had sent me the final list of people who I would be laying off tomorrow. She gave me the script and strongly advised that I stick to it.

Tomorrow would be a hell of a day.

I stood in front of my closet to pick out a blouse to wear for tomorrow. It was really quite convenient that I only needed to dress my top half. My bottom half had been enjoying sweatpants life since we had been quarantined.

I found a monotoned blouse to wear, something not too drab and sad but not too cheery and bright. Then I went to bed early again to ensure that I would be on my game tomorrow. Unfortunately, I had another night of restless sleep. My dreams were just as wacked as the night before and, this time, I just stayed awake from four a.m. on so I would not have to experience those dreams anymore.

My first video call was at nine. I had them scheduled every fifteen minutes. I read from the script, did not divert, and closed the discussion right on time. For most, the shock of the news did not give them the opportunity to truly react. However, there were two, Ben and Colbie, who really shook me. Ben was pure anger. He lashed out at me as if it was all my fault. I couldn't blame him, as he and his wife had just had their third child. But I did feel hurt that he thought that I was to blame. Even though I was hurt by Ben's reaction, Colbie's reaction really rattled me to my core. All she did was smile and say *thank you*.

I thought the last two nights were bad, but nothing compared to the dreams that I had this evening. I fell asleep on the couch and woke myself up crying. My dream had seemed so real. I had been a giant, walking through this little village stomping on houses and people, killing or hurting everyone in sight. And, as I continued my destruction, I could hear a mother screaming at me that this was all my fault. How could I do this to innocent people?

***

Saturday was a normal lockdown weekend—I slept in late. This past week had really taken a toll on me.

Another weekend of hanging around the house, trying to find new and interesting things to do. I went outside to take a brief walk then came right back in. All I did was sleep for the rest of the weekend.

When Monday came, I had to get my head back in the game, as I had the remainder of my team to motivate. I pulled the team together around ten a.m. and officially gave them the news of the layoffs. Their shock quickly turned to fear.

As I was trying my best to keep them calm, a meeting request from Robert popped up on my calendar. I didn't think much of it, since he was probably checking in to see how the conversations had gone and if there had been any problems. Since the meeting was scheduled for ten thirty, I closed the call with my team then checked myself in the mirror to make sure I looked okay for the video call. When I checked the meeting planner again, I realized this was not a video call; he was calling me directly by phone.

The phone rang and, as I thought, Robert asked me how everything had gone and if there had been any problems that he should be aware of. I mentioned Ben, but told him everything otherwise all went as planned. I didn't mention Colbie, as he might not think it was weird.

As I was just about to launch into a number of questions regarding next steps, Robert cleared his throat and robotically started reading *the script*. I went blank. All I could hear was Robert saying, "Thank you for your service." Then the coward hung up.

What the fuck just happened? How could I have gotten laid off? I was a great worker, did what was asked, taking on extra projects, leading a productive team. How the hell could this happen to me? And how dare he take the easy way out and not even look me in the eyes, if only virtually, and tell me to my face? What a wimp. This was so ridiculous. I was going to sue. They couldn't do this to me!

***

I woke up in complete darkness, not knowing if it was morning or night. I looked at the clock. Six thirty. Then I rolled over and picked up my phone from off the floor. What day was it?

What? I had slept for almost an entire day? It was six thirty at night, and I could barely drag myself off the couch.

I went to the kitchen, drank a glass of water, managed to walk up the stairs, and then crawled into bed. I was so tired that I immediately fell back to sleep.

When I finally woke up, it hit me like a ton of bricks.

I don't have a job.

What were people going to say? What was I going to do? How was I going to support myself?

The first tear fell, and I cried for the next hour straight. The truly ugly cry—snot coming out my nose, body convulsing, curled up in the fetal position. I thought the only reason why I stopped was because I was totally dehydrated.

I rolled myself out of the bed, took a shower, pulled on some sweats, and went downstairs ... just to curl up on the couch.

***

Days passed, and all I did was pace around my house, eat, sleep, and cry.

By the second week, Julia, a friend from work, checked in on me.

"So, what are you going to do?" she questioned.

"I don't know. I can barely keep my butt out of bed."

"Why don't you take it easy and think about what you really want to do?"

"What do you mean, *what I really want to do*?"

"Are you trying to tell me you loved your job? It didn't sound like it every week at happy hour." She sighed. "What I mean is, if you could do anything, what would you do?"

"I don't know ... My life was my job."

"Really? You never dreamed about doing something else?" Julia doubted.

"Maybe when I was younger, but I am too old to start over now."

"Please," she scoffed. "Too old? Well, unless you are going to win the lottery, you are eventually going to have to get another job. You might as well do something that you love," she suggested.

After we hung up, her words stayed with me for the rest of the day. What would I do if I could do anything?

Over the next few days, I started to feel more like myself. I only slept eight hours versus twelve, and I showered and got dressed every day. And Julia's words still rang in my head ...

What would I do? This was going to be easy-peasy. I could figure it out. Remember, I was the problem solver, always up for a challenge.

I turned on my computer, opened a clean spreadsheet, and then listed various jobs in the first column—Sales, Marketing, Manager, Ted Talk Speaker, Communications. The second column, I put down if I needed training, and the last column was estimated salary. I then reminded myself that I was an educated woman with years of experience.

"This shouldn't be too hard."

As I worked on my list, Colbie came to mind. I wondered how she was doing, so I worked up the nerve to send her a text, just to say hello and to hope that she and her kids were doing well. No more than ten minutes later, my phone rang. It was Colbie.

Colbie was the only team member—or should I say *former* team member?—who lived in Colorado and actually only lived one town over from me. She was always the levelheaded one. A beautiful woman of mixed races, who I knew was older than me, but you couldn't tell by her looks. Only recently had I noticed that she had started to gray. It probably was the stress of losing her husband, Dan, to cancer, leaving her a single mom, raising her two boys by herself. It seemed like nothing really fazed her. I wished I had that demeanor.

"Colbie, how are you doing?" My voice was filled with concern.

"I guess I could ask you the same thing, Evie," she replied.

"So, you heard."

She softened her voice as she apologetically said, "Yes, and I am sorry."

"What are you sorry about? It happened to you, as well. And I was the one who did it to you."

"You were only the messenger."

"Colbie, the day that I gave you the news, your reaction really rocked me. Can I ask you why you smiled and said *thank you* when I told you that you were laid off?"

"It was time for me to go, anyway. I had known it for a while, but I was too afraid to make the leap," she admitted.

"But, why did you smile? It was as if it didn't bother you at all."

"You may have thought I was speaking to you, but I smiled and said thank you to the Universe because I knew the Universe had other plans for me. Since I was too scared to make the move myself, it gave me a little push."

"Universe?" I scoffed. "You believe in all that kind of stuff?"

"What kind of stuff?" Colbie asked. "Being positive, believing in myself, and knowing that there is more out there than we understand?"

"Well, yeah ... I guess," I replied, trying not to sound too much like a jerk.

"Evie, when was the last time you listened to your heart?"

"You mean, my heartbeat?"

"No, turning off your head—your brain—and listening to your heart. Do you meditate?"

"No, I can't do that. I tried, but I have too much to do, and my mind won't shut down."

"Well, I don't want to sound like an ass to you, but it seems like you have some time on your hands. So, why not try again?"

Her words stung a bit, but she was right.

We said our goodbyes, and she wished me well. Then, before hanging up, Colbie said, "Evie, just trust yourself and follow your heart."

***

Listen to my heart? What does Colbie mean? I asked myself. *How am I supposed to turn off my head?* She said to meditate.

I looked down and noticed that I had been wringing my T-shirt between my fingers. *Maybe I am wound up a little tight*, I thought to myself.

"How hard could this be? I can do this."

Sitting on the living room floor, I clumsily crossed my legs and closed my eyes. Immediately, my eyes popped open, and I got up to check the stove, to make sure I hadn't left it on. Then I went back and sat down.

Okay, second attempt.

I closed my eyes, started deep breathing, and then I heard *drip ... drip ...* The faucet was dripping.

"Ugh, how do people do this?" I asked out loud.

I got up again to turn off the faucet then tried one more time. This time, I took a series of deep breaths, settling in ... when my foot fell asleep.

"Ugh!"

I jumped up, feeling nothing but pins and needles, and hopped around, smacking my foot until the tingling stopped.

"I give up. This is so stupid. I'm not made to do this."

I went to the kitchen to make myself a sandwich and to think about my next move.

"Well, I guess, if I am going to look for a job, I better update my resume and online work profile."

I turned on my laptop and started typing: *Highly competent senior executive, with twenty plus years of experience managing elite sales teams*. Then I wondered if that sounded too brash.

"Nah, it's the truth, and if no one else is going to say it, I might as well."

I saved the overview as a draft so I could think about it some more. Then I decided to go out for a bit, to do some grocery shopping and try to clear my head.

I was just about to drive out of the garage when I realized I had forgotten my mask. *Ugh*. I pulled back in and ran into the house, grabbing my mask then running back out.

Grocery shopping was such a surreal experience these days. Always looking for that extra roll of toilet paper, cleaner, and buying food that I normally would never buy. Plus, it seemed like you couldn't even look at people anymore. Everyone gave each other six feet, trying not to touch anything. And those damn plastic bags? How the hell could you get them open without licking your fingers? All in all, though, the shopping trip wasn't too bad. I had found some good meat, a few treats, a great bottle of wine, and a six-pack of toilet paper.

I took the long way home, keeping the windows open to enjoy the brisk air. It was cold, but the sun was shining. This was the first time in a long time that I felt a little happiness.

I pulled into the garage, grabbed my bags, and then reached into my purse to get my house keys to open the door.

"Where are my house keys?" I asked out loud. I searched my bag, spilling it out on the garage floor. "Fuck. Where are they?" I yelled. I must have left them on the kitchen table when I ran back in to get my mask.

I grabbed my phone and googled a locksmith. Key Lock Locksmith, five stars. I called.

A pleasant-sounding woman answered the phone. "Hello, Key Lock Locksmith."

"Uh, yeah, hi. How long would it take to get someone to 6000 East Pine Way?" I asked. "I locked myself out of the house."

"Um, let me check." There was a momentary pause. "We could get someone out there in about forty-five minutes."

"*Forty-five minutes?* Are you shitting me? Where are you coming from? Boulder?"

"Ma'am, I understand you may be stressed, but that is a soon as I can get someone out there."

"Why would you say I am stressed?" I barked.

"I can hear it in your voice," she replied. "Have you ever tried deep breathing or meditation?"

"What is it with people? You are the second person to say that to me." I paused.

"Would you like me to dispatch a locksmith?" she asked patiently.

"Yes," I sighed out.

"Great. And please remember to have your mask on and give our locksmith six feet. He will also wear a mask and take the necessary safety precautions," she recited. "And, ma'am?"

"Yes?"

"Smile. Life is wonderful." Then she hung up.

"Whatever."

"Forty-five minutes?" I whined. "What am I going to do?" I didn't feel like talking to anyone. I was annoyed and just wanted to be in my house.

I sat in my car and closed my eyes, taking deep breaths. Crazily, I found myself becoming more relaxed. Next thing I knew, I opened my eyes with a start to see the locksmith smiling at me through my car window.

I opened the car door, said hello, and then just let him do his job. It didn't take but a minute for him to open the door.

When he was done, he said, "Isn't meditation great?"

I looked at him with a blank stare, wondering why he would ask me such a question. "What?"

"Don't you just enjoy meditating?" He beamed. "I do it every day. It just puts everything into perspective for me."

"Why would you ask me that? I wasn't meditating," I retorted.

"Oh, I'm sorry. I saw you in such a peaceful state and thought you were meditating. That's why I waited until you opened your eyes."

"I was just trying to relax. Things have been incredibly stressful lately," I told him.

"You could say that again. But life is good. Better to be standing apart six feet than in the ground six feet."

I handed him my credit card, and he swiped it then wiped it down for me before handing it back. We said goodbye, and then he turned back before he left and said, "You should keep doing whatever you think you were doing in the car. You look pretty relaxed. Have a great day."

***

Finally in the house, I dropped my bags on the floor and looked at the kitchen table, fully expecting to see my keys. They weren't there.

What the hell did I do with those keys?

I searched the entire house, but I couldn't find them anywhere. Then, all of a sudden, I heard a soft voice say, *"Check your bag."*

I turned and asked, "What?"

Not knowing what that had been, I ignored it and continued to turn the house upside down.

Again, I heard, *"Check your bag."*

Again, I ignore it.

Then, out of nowhere, I heard as clear as day, *"Evie, check your bag."*

"Fine!" I yelled. To whom? I didn't know.

I found my bag and, as soon as I opened it up, I saw my keys sitting right on top.

"Are you frigging kidding me? They were in my bag the entire time? How did I miss them?" I plopped down in a kitchen chair, hanging my head, and decided I needed to just *slow down.* I was hearing voices. Maybe I was going a little stir-crazy? Maybe I needed to try this meditation thing again?

Once I pulled myself together, I started the process of wiping my groceries down and putting stuff away, thinking to myself, *Why didn't we wipe things down before?* Food traveled from all over the country, and/or world, being touched by who knew who, and I used to just put it in my cupboard or refrigerator without thinking twice? I nodded, knowing I would keep up with this habit once things opened up again.

CHAPTER 2 — RIGHT CHOICE

The next day, the sun was shining, so I decided to try my luck again by meditating outside. I pulled out one of the lawn chairs from the shed and put it directly in the sun. I figured, if I sat in a chair, my foot wouldn't fall asleep, and I would be more apt to *want* to sit quietly in the sun. It truly was a beautiful day, and I found myself in a good place.

A few deep breaths later, I relaxed nicely into the chair. The warmth of the sun on my face made me realize this meditation thing wasn't so bad.

Next thing I knew, my head was flopped to the side, drool escaping from my mouth, and I was sunburned on my cheeks. Guessed I got a little too relaxed, but hey, I seemed to be making progress.

Having a nice nap had given me the energy to start looking for a job. But first, I logged into my bank account to check my balances, wondering how long I actually had before I needed some real income to start coming in.

With unemployment and my savings, I had about nine months before I started tapping into my retirement. That made me consider how buying my grandparents' house on Martha's Vineyard had sounded like a good investment when I'd had a job. I thought it would make me take vacations. Now I wished I had stuck with that little rental place on the Cape.

Sighing with regret, I started my search, using the spreadsheet that I had created a few weeks back. I searched for sales jobs, managerial positions, senior sales executive positions … Not much out there.

Things will start loosening up as this pandemic settles down, I told myself.

My last task of the day was to reach out to my old friend, Hendrix. Maybe he could help me?

"Hendrix Talisman," I spoke into my phone.

Nothing came up in contacts.

Didn't I keep his number? I couldn't find it anywhere, so I went online to google him.

Hendrix Talisman. There you are. Right Choice Professional Search.

He had always wanted to work with me, as he was an up-and-coming headhunter and was constantly asking when I was ready to make a move. I had always thought of him as a Renaissance man, or "the most interesting man in the world," like the commercial, except that he was black and had beautifully coiled dreads.

The phone rang, and then it immediately went to voicemail. *"Hello, you have reached Hendrix at Right Choice Professional Search. I am sorry I cannot come to the phone, but please leave your number and a message, and I will return your call as soon as possible. Thank you, and I look forward to speaking with you."*

"Hello, Hendrix, this is your old friend Evie." I stumbled over my words a little bit and finally was able to spit out, "Well, I am an in need of your services. Please give me a call when you can. Thank you."

My mood was good. I had taken steps to find my next job and had found a great bottle of wine to go with my dinner.

I couldn't say that I was a true extrovert prior to this pandemic, yet I was seriously missing people right now. I guessed I should return some of the texts that I had been ignoring. I just didn't want to talk about it yet. So, I decided against making any type of social effort and cooked myself dinner, with a nice glass of wine.

After dinner, I dove onto the couch and turned on the TV. It seemed like I had streamed and binge-watched every show I had ever liked. And I couldn't do reruns again, so I called it a night.

Sleep had been coming easier than it had ever had when I had been working. It always seemed like I had been stressing over something and would wake up at two thirty in the morning. Now I slept all night and wasn't having any more wacked-out dreams.

For some reason, my bed felt extra comfortable tonight. And, as I was drifting off, I thought about the voice that I thought I had heard.

"It was nothing," I told myself. "I am here, all by myself, so how could I hear voices? Stress. It's got to be stress."

***

Early in the morning, I rolled over, kind of awake but not really. Knowing I didn't have anything to do, I rolled back over to get more sleep. And, as I drifted off, I began to dream and heard, *"Evie, listen to your heart, listen to your heart ..."*

After a restful sleep, I made myself some coffee and scrambled a few eggs.

Scrolling through the news, I remembered my dream. Something about listening to my heart? *What is all this stuff about listening to my heart? What does it mean?* I wondered.

My phone rang.

"Evie, how are you doing? How are things?" Hendrix asked in his smooth, deep voice

"Hi, Hendrix. Thanks for calling me back. I wanted to let you know that I would love to use your services."

"What?"

"Yup, I got laid off a number of weeks ago. Had a nice little rest, and now I'm ready to hit it hard," I told him.

"Wow, okay. What type of work are you looking for? But, before you answer, I do want you to know it's not a normal job market. Things are really tight," he said.

"I figured as much, but I have a little time to find the right opportunity."

"Great. Send me your resume, job requirements, and salary, and I will get to work."

"Wonderful! And thank you." I guessed my *thank you* sounded a little more desperate than I wanted.

"Of course." He paused. "Are you okay?"

"Yes … well, no. It's been hard. I never thought I would be here at this age."

"Don't worry, sweetheart; we will find you your dream job. Speaking of, what is your dream job?"

I sighed. "You are the second person to ask me that question. How am I supposed to know?"

"Well, I can find you another sales job, but why work so hard when you didn't really like the last one? If you are going to exert energy, shouldn't it be toward something you love? Think about it. Listen to your heart, and you will know."

I slapped the table, demanding, "What is this? A conspiracy? Why is everyone telling me to listen to my heart?"

"Whoa, whoa … Because your heart is the real you. It tells you your truths."

"I'm sorry, but I just don't understand what you all mean. *The real me? My truth*? Hendrix, you know me. What you see is what you get," I boasted.

"Really?"

"Yes, really!" I assured.

"Okay, then. Send me your job requirements tomorrow, and I will get right on it."

"Thank you, Hendrix. Sorry to be so jumpy. I really appreciate your help."

***

I poured myself a third cup of coffee then sat down to write my dream job description.

What would I want to do if I could do anything?

Nothing was coming to me while sitting down, so I changed the scenery by walking around the house, asking this question over and over again. *What would I want to do if I could do anything? What would I want to do if I could do anything?*

Finally, I threw my hands up in the air and asked out loud, "Why is this so hard?" I had always known what I wanted to do. I had always had a direction, a blueprint of what I wanted next, but now I couldn't answer the simple question of: *what was my dream job?* Could there really be a dream job? If it was a job, then it must be work. I wondered if I just didn't want to work anymore. Yes, it would be nice to not work, but then how could I retire? I needed to make more money to retire in the way I really wanted.

"Ugh! Why am I so confused?" I yelled.

I simply didn't know what I wanted.

I started to breathe faster and faster, shorter and shorter breaths. I felt like I was going to pass out. I bent over, trying to steady myself. *What the hell is happening to me?*

I fell to the floor, gasping for air. Then I crawled over to the couch and propped myself up against it, telling myself, "Breathe, Evie, breathe." I closed my eyes and tried to take a deeper breath, repeatedly telling myself to calm down. "Breathe, breathe, breathe."

Finally, I began to breathe normally. Then I slumped over and started to cry. *What is going on with me?*

Once I got my strength back, I crawled up on the couch and stared at the ceiling. "Am I having a nervous breakdown? Why am I falling apart?" I lay there, just staring at the ceiling. "What am I going to do?"

First, I need to switch to decaf, I thought to myself.

I snickered then heard a voice say, *"Listen to your heart."*

Oh shit, I really was going crazy. I kept hearing voices.

I lay there a little longer then quietly asked, "Am I going crazy?"

"*No.*"

"Then who is talking to me?"

"*I am you, and you are me.*"

"What? Who is this?" I asked nervously.

"*I am you.*"

Okay, I really was losing it. I couldn't even understand the voice in my head. I needed to talk to someone real. I had obviously been alone for too long. But who?

Just then, my phone rang.

"Oh, Hendrix, I am so glad you called," I answered in a hurry, so glad to hear a voice that wasn't "*I am you, and you are me.*"

"Evie, what's up?" he asked. "You sound frazzled."

"Okay," I sighed out nervously. "We are friends, right?"

"Of course."

"Please don't hold this against me, 'cause this is going to sound really weird."

"Don't worry," he assured.

Slowly, I told him, "I have been hearing voices in my head." I proceeded to tell him about the house key incident and my dream job breakdown.

He stayed quiet for a little while before he let out a slight chuckle. "Oh, Evie, that is your higher self talking to you."

"My what?" I asked, bewildered.

"Your higher self, God, The Source, Spirit. It goes by many names," he explained.

In awe, I asked, "Hendrix, how do you know this?"

Then I said to myself, *Of course he knows this. He is the most interesting man in the world.* I smiled at my own joke.

"Because I speak with my higher self all the time," he responded.

"And it talks back?" I teased.

He laughed. "Yes, it talks back. That is what I was alluding to when I said *listen to your heart.* Most people let their brain run the show. However, it is your heart that should guide you. Your heart tells you what you need to know. It reminds you of who you truly are, and it always tells you the truth, unlike your brain."

"Hendrix, this is sounding really weird and way out there."

"I guess it does, but please don't be scared. What has happened to you is amazing. There is so much ahead of you to experience. I am so excited for you."

"So, why am I feeling so confused and weird?" I questioned.

"Because you have finally quieted your mind and started to ask yourself real questions. Real questions about your true self. Now that you have asked these questions, you have to be quiet and listen for the answer."

"Are you telling me that, if I ask a question and listen, I will hear the answer?" I repeated.

"Yes."

"So, I can ask for this week's Powerball number, and I will receive it?"

He hesitated. "Yes, that *could* happen, but that's a tall order for your first question. Why don't you start with the question you already asked: what is your dream job?"

"Okay. I can do that ... I think." I hesitated for a few then said, "Hendrix, thank you for being so open and not thinking I am losing my mind."

"Don't worry, sweetheart; I have been there. At first, I also thought I was crazy. You're not. You have just discovered one of the many wonders of the Universe. Call me anytime, and don't worry about getting me the information tomorrow. I think you need some more time."

CHAPTER 3 — HIGHER SELF

Why was I so scared to ask that question? It was a simple enough question. *I probably wouldn't hear an answer, anyway,* I thought.

What am I thinking? If Hendrix can do it, then so can I ... right?

I went outside to clear my head, walking around the backyard, inspecting for any signs of spring. I hoped my flowers started to sprout soon, but we could get snow here up until May, *so stay warm and dry, little flowers. You have another few months.*

Thinking about spring put me in a better place, and I finally made the decision to ask the question.

I went back inside, grabbed a glass of water, and sat at the kitchen table. I sat up straight and formal, as if my higher self was sitting across from me. Then I cleared my throat. "So, higher self, I'm Evie. Oh, but I guess you know that already. Hendrix said that I'm supposed to ask you what my perfect job is and that you will tell me. So, here it goes. Higher self, what is my perfect job?"

I sat and waited ... and waited.

Nothing.

I waited a little longer.

Still nothing.

I looked up to the ceiling. "I'm listening. How come you're not saying anything now?" *When I don't want to hear you, I do. But, when I do, you have nothing to say?*

I knew this was crazy. It might work for Hendrix, but it surely wasn't working for me.

I pushed myself away from the table with a huff. I didn't even know why I was so mad. I *knew* this was crazy. I just needed to think about this some more, and I could figure it out by myself. I always did.

I felt the need to start cleaning, which I could admit I didn't do often.

I walked down the hall to the junk room. Since I couldn't go to the gym, I could turn this into my home gym. I pushed the door open and became instantly overwhelmed.

"How did I get so much stuff?" I asked myself aloud.

I walked out, thinking I couldn't handle that mess now, but something made me want to turn back.

"Fine, let's start small."

I walked back into the room, looking for the smallest box to go through.

Ooo ... that's a good one.

As I leaned over, I knocked over a few boxes, and all my old painting stuff fell out onto the floor.

"Crap, look at this mess."

I gathered all the brushes, putting them back into their case. Following the narrow pathway through the room, I then noticed a few canvases leaning up against the wall. As I thumbed through them, I found a half-started painting. *Hey, this isn't too bad.*

As I stared at the painting, I wondered why I had ever stopped. I used to love getting caught up in all the colors, being outside, painting sceneries, but painting didn't pay the bills.

I put the canvas back, grabbed the small box, and brought it back to the kitchen.

What is this stuff? Pens, staplers, junk. *Geez, this is from my old desk, two jobs ago.*

I removed the stapler and threw the rest into the trash. *Hmm, that felt rather good.*

I went back in and looked for another box.

As I was squeezing through, I slammed my knee into my old painting easel. "Argh!" Shit, that hurt.

I picked the easel up, running my fingers over the worn wood. This used to be my grandmother's easel. Just thinking about her brought a smile to my face. She had been an amazing artist. No formal training; just pure, natural talent. I had always hoped to be as good of a painter as her, but it hadn't worked out. I had needed to make a living.

My grandparents had basically raised me and played integral roles in my life. My grandmother gave me the love of painting, and my grandfather the dedication to work hard.

I pulled the easel, canvases, paints, and brushes all out, stacking them up in the living room. Maybe I could sell these? They were still in fairly good shape.

I sauntered back into the junk room and cleaned out a few more boxes, so now there was a real walkway into the room. Purging felt really awesome. Somehow, I felt lighter.

Enough for now, tomorrow was another day. I wanted to really cook tonight. But, what to have?

As I looked in the refrigerator, I heard, "Salmon with a side salad."

Wait—had I said that, or had I heard it?

Great, now I couldn't even trust my own hearing.

Regardless, I was feeling fantastic. Music on, a great glass of wine, and I was cooking like a real champ. The house smelled delicious, too. *Let's do this up!*

I put a setting for one at the dining room table and enjoyed my wonderfully cooked salmon with a perfectly dressed salad.

I glanced over at my painting stuff again, wonderful memories of my first show flooding back into my mind. Grandma had been so proud of me, even though she had only been one of a handful who had shown up. It hadn't mattered to her; she had just been happy that I had taken the chance, put myself out there, and let people see the real me.

Humph, the real me.

I didn't know if it was the wine or the music, but I got the urge to paint.

Rummaging through the junk room, I found the drop cloth. Then I set myself up in the living room to look out the window for inspiration. My paints had survived ... kind of. I took out a few tubes, put some paint onto my palette, and began to mix.

As I swiped the brush into the paint, I got a tingling sensation on the top right side of my head.

"Whoa." I guessed I'd had more wine than I had thought.

Painting was like riding a bicycle. I got into the flow immediately. It was such a freeing experience. I floated through the night, painting nonstop. When I paused to look at what I had done and to grab another sip of wine, I realized it was three in the morning. Smiling, I recalled how I would always lose track of time when I painted.

Let's call it a night.

Looking around, I noticed how much of a mess I had made of myself. Paint was all over me. So, I closed things up, meticulously cleaned my brushes, and then headed for the shower.

The water felt amazing. Each droplet hitting my skin felt like it was electrified. I normally became relaxed when I showered, but tonight, I could feel energy running through me. When I was done, I got out, dried off, and then pulled a sleep shirt on. It was all I could do to brush my teeth before I passed out.

***

At almost ten a.m.—*boy, that was some good wine*—I headed into the kitchen and made some coffee. Then, as I waited, I walked into the living room to turn on the news. There, against the wall, sitting on Grandma's easel, was one of the best paintings I had ever painted. I just stood there and stared, looking at the details, the colors, the composition.

I need to buy more of that wine, I thought to myself.

I was lost in my thoughts when I heard my phone ringing from the bedroom.

Running up the stairs, I lunged for the phone, slid onto the bed, and picked up just before I crashed onto the floor on the other side.

"Hello?" I said on a laugh, half out of breath.

"Evie? Well, you sound better," Hendrix complimented.

"Hey, Hendrix."

"I was just calling to check in on you. I wanted to make sure I didn't freak you out."

I laughed and told him, "No, you didn't freak me out too much. But I did want to tell you that I asked the question, but I didn't hear an answer. So, I guess it doesn't work for me."

"Don't give up. Sometimes you have to give it time."

"Well, it's out there, but I'm not waiting. I can figure this out on my own. Hey, do you still drink wine?"

"A little. Why?" he asked.

"I had this amazing bottle last night. It was so good that it got me back into painting. I painted the most amazing picture last night, thanks to that wine."

"Hold up. You did what last night?" he interrupted. "I didn't know you knew how to paint?"

I gave Hendrix a quick recap of what had happened, but he kept on stopping me, asking for more details.

"Why are you so interested in what happened?" I probed.

"Do you not realize that you *did* receive your answer?" he asked in a way that sounded like a declaration.

"What? But I didn't hear anything."

"You don't always. Sometimes, you are shown. And it seems like, with you, you had to do. Your perfect job is to be an artist, a painter," he proclaimed.

"I tried that once, Hendrix, but I realized I needed to eat. I'm not doing that again."

"All right. But, just remember how you felt when you were painting. You, yourself, said that was the best painting you had ever done. When you listen to your heart and follow it, life becomes easier, more joyful, and you discover you can do things you never thought you could do before. Trust me.

"How do you think I got into this business?" he asked. "You remember how I used to sell software? I hated going to work every day. I listened to my heart and heard that I was a good connector. I like people, and I like connecting them. I also have a good business acumen and can sell anything. Thus, this opportunity was provided, and I took the leap. Now look at me. I am number one in my office again this month, and I am thinking about going out on my own. I would have never dreamed that I could do all that I am doing now."

I heard Hendrix, and I was honestly incredibly happy for him, but I told him again, "I tried this once before, and it didn't work. Why would it work now?"

"Evie, this is the last thing I am going to say: it will work now because you are open to hearing your heart, and if you follow, utterly amazing things will happen." Then he reminded me, "Send me your job requirements whenever you want to."

"Thanks, Hendrix."

"Don't thank me. Thank yourself."

When we hung up, I got up from the floor and hobbled back to the kitchen to get my coffee.

As I walked into the living room, I saw my painting again. Could I be a full-time artist?

I stood there, reveling in the idea, but then I snapped myself out of it.

Wake up, Evie. That was a hard life. You never knew if you could pay the rent or if you had enough money for food. Grandma isn't here anymore.

Then I heard my grandfather's words, loud and clear. "*Evie, it's time to grow up and get a job.*"

***

After breakfast, I threw on some sweats then went back to cleaning the junk room. Who knew? If I got this cleaned out, I could actually have a home gym.

Somehow, I was able to clean out another five boxes before lunch.

Damn, I was on a roll.

"Seriously, how did I get so much stuff?" I asked myself again.

If it were a different time, I could have held a huge garage sale. Instead, I was separating clothes, household items, and books for donation. Most of the rest would get thrown away.

Patting myself on the back, I left the room, knowing I had accomplished a lot today. I could actually see an entire wall now!

Tomorrow was garbage day, so I started organizing what I would throw out. I no longer needed that desk chair, so I rolled it down the driveway.

When I turned to walk back to the house, a car pulled up. The driver, a young Asian woman, rolled down the window and asked, "Excuse me. Are you throwing out that chair?"

"Yes, I am."

"Does it work?"

"Yes, I just got a new one. This one is perfectly fine," I told her with a smile.

"May I take it?" she asked politely.

"Of course."

"Yes!" She parked the car and got out.

As she walked toward me, she said, "I knew something amazing was going to happen to me today when I was told to turn down this street. I asked the Universe last week for a new desk chair since I am working from home and my kitchen chair hurts my back. I don't have the extra money to buy one, so this is simply perfect."

I looked at her inquisitively. "You were told to drive down this street?"

"Yeah, sort of. Don't you ever get that feeling when you just *have* to do something? I was actually heading in the exact opposite direction, but I felt the need to be on *this* street, and now I know why. Thank you so much! You have made my day," she exclaimed.

"No worries." I waved her off.

As she put the chair in her car, she said, "By the way, my name is Triniti. Thanks again, and have a great day!"

"You as well," I responded as she pulled away from the curb. Then I thought to myself, *That was really interesting.* I guessed more people than I thought believed in that stuff.

Climbing the stairs to go back into the house, I saw my next-door neighbor, Sue. That woman was a real piece of work. She was always in everyone's business and believed her poop didn't stink. I could only handle her in small doses.

"Hey, Evie. How are you doing? I noticed you have been out and about more. Work isn't keeping you busy?" she observed.

"Actually, Sue, I was laid off."

Whoa, I couldn't believe I had just said that so matter-of-factly.

"Oh no, Evie, sorry to hear that. What are you going to do?"

"Just taking my time to figure out my next move."

"Wow, you seem pretty calm. I would be freaking out. I can't imagine not having a job. I check my bank account every week as it is. Not having money coming in would put me into a tailspin," she carried on. "Well, good luck. I hope you find something soon."

"Thanks ... I think."

Back inside the house, I felt proud of myself that I had been able to talk about being laid off without feeling ashamed. However, now I felt compelled to check my bank account.

I logged on through my phone and sat on the floor. *Huh, I thought I had more savings than that.*

I started to freak a little, thinking, *I need to get my information over to Hendrix by the end of the week!*

Now depressed, I collected the rest of the stuff that I was going to throw out then brought it to the curb.

The room looked great now, changing my mood again to one of accomplishment. I had forgotten how much sunshine the room received through the nice big window. Such a wonderful view. I stacked the remaining boxes in the corner, thinking I would deal with them tomorrow.

It was really nice having this extra time to do things that I had been needing to do. Unfortunately, it also gave me the time to think. And I had to admit that, since I had talked to Sue, my financial situation worried me more. If I created a budget and cut back, I could probably squeeze out an extra couple of months. Paying a mortgage for a property that I wouldn't be able to visit until who knew when was also giving me agita.

CHAPTER 4 — MEDITATE

"If you don't call me, I am sending the police over," flashed across my phone screen.

I loved Reva, but she was a bit of a drama queen. We had known each other since college. She was a wonderful person, with beautiful, perfect brown skin, a huge smile, and eyes that always sparkled. She was so caring of everyone, but she'd had some hard knocks in life. I admired her. She seemed to always land on her feet with a smile on her face. She would give someone her last dollar if she knew they needed it. Sometimes, she was my best friend, and other times, she served as my surrogate mother. I guessed she was in mother mode today.

I poured myself a seltzer and got comfortable on the couch. I was in for a *long* conversation.

When the phone rang, I picked it up.

"It's about time. I was about to do a sanity check on you!" Reva screamed.

"Hello, Reva, how are you?"

"I'm fine, but what about you? Where have you been?" she asked accusingly.

"I've been here."

"So ..." She paused.

"Sew buttons," I responded, a term my grandmother always said, and I knew Reva hated it. She always said it didn't make any sense.

"Evie, how are you?" she asked. "I have been worried sick about you. You went complete radio silence. This pandemic has us all acting weird, but I haven't heard from you in *weeks*."

I told Reva about being laid off and that I had just been trying to get my head back on straight so I could figure out my next move.

"No wonder you went silent. That's a shitty thing to go through. I feel like I have been there too many times," she responded. "I hope you are taking some time to be thoughtful about your next move. Don't jump into something just to get paid. Life isn't about money."

"I have heard, from so many people, to listen to my heart, to do what I love, blah, blah, blah. That's all nice and good, but I do have bills, and I need to make money!" I exclaimed.

"I know, I know. You are preaching to the choir. But remember, you can do what you love and *still* make money."

"Yeah, so they say."

"What do you think, that all those movie stars, artists, writers, singers, and businesspeople you follow on social media were just lucky? No. It took work, focus, and a belief in themselves. They believed they would succeed in doing what they loved, and they did," she stated.

"Yeah, well, maybe I have more bills than they do," I retorted.

"Evie, seriously. Do you want for anything? Are you hungry? Do you sleep out in the cold? Are you sick?

"No, no, and no."

"So, what are you worried about? You are wealthy in so many ways. Believe me; money is nice, and we all need it, but if you are happy, healthy, are surrounded by people you love and who love you, what else do you need? You can't take it with you." She paused. "Evie, are you listening?"

I rolled my eyes. "Yes."

"Don't start believing you don't have enough. That kind of thinking puts your energy in lack. When you believe you don't have, you are ultimately right. Know that you have abundance in your life and more will come. That's just how energy works. I know you are rolling your eyes and saying under your breath, *Yes, Mother*, but this shit is real! How do you think I have been able to bounce back so many times?"

"I'm not rolling my eyes," I lie.

"Whatever. I will leave you with one of my favorite quotes by Charlie Wardle. *A bird sitting in a tree is never afraid of the branch breaking because its trust is not in the branch, but in its own wings.* Think about it, Evie. I will check in again next week, and you better answer your phone!" she warned.

"Yes, Mother," I said in the most loving way.

"*Hmph.* I love you, Evie."

"I love you, too."

When we hung up, I started to think about what this pandemic had done to people. Everything was so different.

I needed to eat!

I made myself a peanut butter and honey sandwich with a glass of milk. Easy-peasy, has protein, and I am too mentally drained from the day to do much else. I ate dinner in front of the TV, watching the cooking channel. Not a good idea when you were eating a PB&H, but there was nothing else on. Then I headed to bed, so mentally drained that I fell right to sleep.

***

At around two thirty in the morning, I rolled over and heard, "*Why do you think you have to do this all by yourself?*"

Huh? I couldn't tell if I was awake or dreaming.

"*If you follow me, you will live the life you desire. Meditate in the morning, and you will learn more.*"

Is this really happening?

I thought this had to be a dream and fell back to sleep.

***

I sat up in bed, put my pillows behind my back, and crossed my legs.

Meditate, and I will learn more. I remembered hearing.

I hadn't tried to meditate since the sunburn incident. I guessed this was as good a time as any to try again. For some reason, I was looking forward to trying again. *All right, here we go.*

I closed my eyes and took some deep breaths.

As I sat, I heard, *"Just breathe."*

It felt like I was sitting and breathing forever when I eventually heard, *"You are loved, you are beautiful, you are amazing."*

I didn't know what that was, but it felt fantastic, causing a smile to break out across my face.

Then I heard, *"Believe and know this is real. Ask and you shall be answered. I am here for you."*

After another minute or two, I opened my eyes. Whatever that was, I liked it … a lot. I felt so good and energized. If this was what meditation was, I would keep doing it.

Even as the day progressed, I felt lighter, happier. I would dare say I even felt joy. It had been a long time since I could say that.

I decided to purchase a yoga mat and meditation pillow. If I was going to do this, I might as well do it right, right? Then I went into the junk room and started looking around to see what I could do with this space. There was definitely enough room for my exercise equipment, meditation stuff, and I could probably fit my easel and paint supplies in here, as well. I felt wonderful, like my life was coming back together.

To not waste that feeling, I sat on the floor and texted Hendrix my job requirements.

1) Six figure salary
2) Executive level
3) Travel (after pandemic)
4) Ability to work from home
5) Ability to create
6) Sales and/or marketing

That should give him enough to start a search. I would be working in no time.

Hendrix acknowledged receipt of the text with a thumbs-up.

The remainder of the week, I found myself wanting to be outside more, so I found excuses to take walks, go grocery shopping, and just sit out in the backyard. It wasn't spring yet, but the sun was always shining in Colorado.

***

For the past few days, I couldn't get Colbie out of my mind. I had been feeling a little stir-crazy, so I texted her to see if she would like to meet for a socially distant coffee. She came back quickly, saying that I had been on her mind a lot lately, as well. We then planned to meet at over at Red Barn Park.

We both showed up with coffees and masks.

"Colbie, so good to see you," I greeted. "It seems like forever."

"I wish I could hug you. I missed you, Evie. Wow, what have you done with yourself?" she commented.

"What do you mean?"

"You are glowing, even under your mask. I can see a twinkle in your eyes. Did you meet someone?"

"No, I wish," I scoffed. "I guess it's the slower pace and the constant eight hours of sleep."

Relationships were the one thing that had always eluded me. I was always up for a challenge, but when it came to men, I just didn't know what they wanted. Most of the time, I felt like I was competing with them in work, so I didn't know how to turn it off when I was in a social setting. Just as well, as I didn't have time, anyway. The same reason why I never got a dog.

"Well, whatever it is, keep on doing it."

We walked over to a bench, and Colbie sat down at one end, and I at the other.

Colbie then jumped in and said, "It's been really weird. You have crossed my mind a number of times over the past few days. It almost felt like you were calling me, just not over the phone.

So, when I got your text, I made sure to make time." She took a sip of her coffee, her head angled as if she were studying me. "So ... what's up?"

"I have been thinking a lot about you, as well, so yes, I guess I have been calling you. A lot of crazy things have been happening lately, and since you believe in that stuff ..." I trailed off.

"You mean, spirituality?" Colbie articulated.

"Yes, spirituality. I thought you can explain some things to me."

"Sure, I will do the best I can, but please know that everyone's experience is different, and I still learn every day."

I nodded then went into my explanation. "So, I have been hearing voices when I'm asleep, as well as when I am awake. Last week, I had a dream that said the voice is real, and if I ask questions, I will receive answers. Oh, I was also told that, if I follow what the voice says, I will live the life that I desire."

"Nice!" she exclaimed, her eyes twinkling.

I threw my hands up in exasperation. "*Nice?* That's all you have to say? This isn't weird to you?"

"No, it's magnificent. You have awakened."

Feeling like a dog hearing a new sound, I tilted my head and raised my eyebrow. "Huh? What does that mean?"

"You have allowed yourself to remember that you have a higher self, an energy that is all knowing. Some people call it God. Personally, I like to call it Spirit. Do you believe there is something greater than yourself out there?"

I nodded. "Yes, I guess ... but I haven't really given it much thought. I am not a religious person."

"Nor am I, but I am spiritual," she explained. "I won't try to explain everything, mainly because I can't, but what I will say is that everything is energy, even inanimate objects. Energy attracts energy. So, if you are happy and your energy is high, you are more likely to attract happy people and see more beauty. But, if you are mad and your energy is low, you will attract unhappy people and unfortunate things may happen. Just like when you are mad and running late, inevitably, you can't find your keys, or you stub your toe rushing around. Energy attracts energy."

"I can see that, but why am I hearing voices?" I muttered.

"Is it voices or just one?"

I didn't answer immediately. "Huh, I think it's just one."

"Well, this could be Spirit or an angel. You will need to ask."

"Ask?" I responded frantically.

"Yes, ask. Please, you were a senior executive at a fortune 500, and you are afraid to ask who you are talking with?" she scoffed. "Once you find out, we can speak again. But I do think that you should read some books to learn more. Meditation—however you do it—is one of the best ways to connect to your higher self."

"What do you mean, *however I do it?*" I asked. "I thought you had to sit cross-legged, eyes closed, deep breathing."

"Well, that's one way," Colbie said. "But people meditate in many ways. You can do it however you want. Just be open-minded and focused. If other thoughts come into your head, let them pass through. If they try to stay around, focus on your breathing, and they will move on. It takes practice. But don't get all weird about it. Have fun, relax. You can also listen to music, if it helps."

"So, does everyone know about this?" I probed.

She shook her head. "No, not really."

"So, I can't bring this up in everyday conversation with anyone?"

"You can, but not everyone will understand. I know it is confusing and exciting all rolled up in one and, to be honest, sometimes it can be lonely. You are experiencing things that not everyone can or wants to. You can reach out to me anytime, but you will find your people. I would start with happy people, because they see life in a different way."

I sat there, trying to make sense of it all. Spirit, angels, energy, voices? It was almost too much to handle. I spent my entire life staying away from religion, mainly because it didn't make sense. People preached love and forgiveness, then some of those same people would spew hate and hurt children. I knew that could be viewed as an over generalization, but the church had hurt way too many people throughout history, and I wanted nothing to do with it.

Colbie stared at me. "You're thinking. What is going through your head right now?"

"This is a lot to take in, and I am not all that comfortable with it. When you talk about angels and God or Spirit, how is spirituality any different than religion?"

Colbie closed her eyes, as if to collect her thoughts. "That's a big question. Some would say that religion is based on a set of organized beliefs that are used to unite a group of people, and spirituality is an individual belief that focuses on the soul. My personal opinion is that religion is based on a God, or Spirit, that is outside of the individual. Spirituality believes that God, or Spirit, is within the individual and that we are all connected."

"Huh, I never thought of it that way. That makes much more sense to me."

We sat in silence for a few minutes before I said, "Colbie, this has been so nice. I have missed social interaction, and I have missed your wisdom. You probably gave me a lot of good nuggets of wisdom over the years, but I guess I did not hear as clearly back then," I admitted.

"Oh, that brings up something else that you should know. Ego," Colbie added.

"What about it?"

"We all have it," Colbie explained, "some more than others. It is there to protect you, though it is based on fear and past experiences. You are learning to live in the present. Ego can't control the present, but it can make you think it controls the past and future. Just think, when you have anxiety, generally, it is about what you think is going to happen. Ego is right there, saying you can't because it didn't work in the past, so it won't happen in the future. When you listen to ego, you have limits. When you listen to your heart, there are no limits. Ego has been in control for a long time. You could say it has gotten you far, but your life can be much easier, and you can reach heights that you never expected, if you let go of ego and only listen to your heart," she explained.

"Funny you should say that," I joked. "I think ego and I have been commiserating a bit more lately."

"Just remember, ego does not play fair. The sooner you realize it is your ego, the quicker you can put it in its place and start listening to you heart," she advised. "Don't try to understand this all at once. It takes time, and you will continue to meet people who will give you more wisdom. Just know you have a gift—we all do—and we are being asked to share it. To share our true selves and to love. Enjoy this ride. That's why we are all here on Earth—to experience and enjoy life."

"Colbie, thank you! I feel so peaceful talking to you," I told her.

"You're welcome. When I get home, I will send the titles of a few books that will help you understand more," she promised.

"Colbie," I stopped her before she left, "I wanted to ask: how are you doing? Losing your job couldn't have been easy."

She smiled. "Oh, we are great. We are wealthier than my bank account may suggest. There is something amazing on my horizon, I know it."

"Well, if you need anything, please let me know."

"Thank you, Evie. I really appreciate that."

I looked at Colbie with my arms open and asked, "Can we?"

"Of course."

We hugged for a long time. It felt like we both needed it. Then we headed in opposite directions.

Walking back to my car, I had a bit more pep in my step, so instead of going right back home, I decided to take a walk around the park and experience the beauty.

CHAPTER 5 — PAINT YOUR FEELINGS

A couple of months had passed since I had been laid off, and a lot had changed for me. I had been meditating regularly and generally feeling calmer, happier, and more inspired. I no longer went into radio silence and actually had been reaching out to people more. The pandemic restrictions were starting to ease up, and more people seemed to be out. I was feeling rather good about myself and my life.

The weather had been getting better, and I had the urge to paint again. I hadn't touched my brushes since I had created my painting under what I thought was the "influence of a great bottle of wine." Today's adventure would be done completely sober and out in public.

I grabbed my supplies, a clean canvas, and Grandma's easel then headed out to Red Barn Park where Colbie and I had met for coffee. The experience with her at the park had been so wonderful that I thought I would paint the barn and give it to her as a thank you for her guidance.

Just as I was packing up the car, my phone pinged. It was Hendrix with a couple of opportunities that he wanted me to look at. This news sent a shiver down my spine. I didn't know if I was happy or anxious, so I decided to deal with it after my excursion to the park.

The park seemed pretty quiet. Only a few families with small children ran around. Everything had been more quiet than usual since the pandemic.

I found a great spot with a perfect view of the barn and set everything up. The sun was perfect, casting a wonderful glow over the barn.

I took a deep breath and was just about to begin painting when a little girl came running over.

"Whatcha doing?" she questioned in a cute lisp-y voice.

"Huh? Oh, I'm going to paint a picture." I smiled at her.

"Of what?" she asked.

"Of this barn."

She pouted. "Oh ... That sounds boring."

"Really? I think the barn is beautiful."

"It needs animals. All barns have animals," she proclaimed.

"Well, this painting will hopefully remind a friend of a wonderful time we had together, sitting on that bench in front of the barn," I explained, pointing toward the bench.

"What kind of animals are you going to paint?" she responded.

I looked at her, puzzled, and said, "I'm not going to paint any animals because there are none here."

"Oh yes, there are! I see a horse sticking his head out of the barn, a cat sitting on the fence, cleaning its paw, and a pig bathing in the mud."

I smiled. "Wow, you have a very vivid imagination. How do you see all those animals?"

"I don't see them. I just know they are there," she bragged.

Suddenly, a frantic woman called in the distance, "Sammy! Sammy, where are you?"

"Over here, Mommy!" the little girl replied.

The mother came rushing over. "Sammy, please don't leave my sight. You had me worried."

She then turned to me and said, "I am so sorry about this. I hope she didn't bother you."

"No, and no worries. Your daughter has a very vivid imagination. I bet she is an amazing little artist. Her creativity is wonderful, and she has definitely made me see things in a different light."

"Yes, Sammy is highly creative. She sees things that the rest of us just can't. She brings a whole new perspective to all of us," her mother shared.

I knelt down to look Sammy in the eyes. "Well, Sammy, it was wonderful to meet you, and thank you for opening my eyes."

She grinned. "You're welcome."

After Sammy and her mother left, I noticed the sun had moved, causing a glare to be cast on the barn, so I decided to call it a day and packed up my stuff.

When I got home, I brought everything in and dropped it in the living room. Then I got caught up looking at my phone when I heard, *"Paint."*

"Paint? I missed the opportunity, and I need to do a few other things," I said out loud.

I sat down to pay some bills when I again heard, *"Paint."*

"Fine," I said. "I'll paint."

I set myself up facing the window. As I looked out, trying to decide what to paint, I was told, *"Paint the barn."*

"How am I to paint the barn? I'm not there, and I didn't take a photo!" I yelled, feeling exasperated.

"Feel the barn and paint it."

"Feel it?" I said even louder.

"Close your eyes and remember how you felt at the barn. Paint your feelings."

I hesitated, looked around the room as if to see if anyone was looking, then decided, "What the hell? I'll try it."

I closed my eyes, remembering the feeling of calm that Colbie always gave me. Her words gave me peace and positive energy. It was a beautiful, crisp day. I could feel the sun …

When I opened my eyes, I began to paint. Each stroke was effortless. The colors magnificent. Images appeared that had not been there, at the barn, but I could *feel* them. I poured my feelings into the painting, something I had never done before. It was a fascinating experience.

When I stepped back, all I saw was love. I loved how it looked. I loved how it made me feel.

I was so excited that I immediately texted Colbie, asking if I could swing by her house tomorrow to drop something off.

"What is happening?" I asked myself. "How am I able to do this? Where is this coming from?" I stared at the painting some more, soaking in all the colors.

Colbie texted me back, saying she would be in and out all day, but she would leave the screen door unlocked, and I could leave it in the door if she wasn't home.

I sat on the floor, looking at the painting again. In that moment, I realized that this was what happened when I listened to my higher self. This was what it meant for life to become easier, to see more beauty.

I closed my eyes and said, "Thank you."

***

The following day, I wrapped the painting then jumped into my car to drive over to Colbie's. She owned a cute ranch that screamed, "I have children," since there were bikes and sports equipment strewn across the front yard.

Pulling into the driveway, I gave a quick honk to see if anyone was home. When no one responded, I slipped the painting between the screen door and taped a note to the front door.

As I started to back out of the driveway, I heard a honk. Colbie was just returning.

Smiling, I rolled down my window and told her, "I left the gift between the doors."

"Do you have time?" Colbie probed.

"Sure." I nodded, wondering why she asked. "I'll wait in the car."

Colbie gave a little wave then pulled into the garage. Not a minute later, she came through the front door, and I watched as she unwrapped the painting. Then all I heard was a gasp.

"Evie, this is absolutely stunning. Did you paint this?"

"Yes. I wanted to say thank you for the guidance you gave me when we met at the park," I told her.

"I didn't know you were so talented. The colors and the image are so peaceful. I love your interpretation of the moment."

I smiled. "Thank you. I received my inspiration from a little girl named Sammy."

"Congratulations. This is truly magnificent. Have you ever thought of selling your work?"

"I tried a long time ago, but it didn't work out. I just do it for fun now," I explained.

"Well, you should really think about trying again. Your work is utterly amazing. Actually, I have a friend who works with artists to get their pieces purchased or placed into office buildings, restaurants, and other places. She also helps artists market and host shows. I would be happy to pass along her information. I am sure she would be extremely interested in your work," she offered.

"Thank you, Colbie, but, as I said, I am just doing this for fun. I need to find myself a real job. I have a couple of leads, too, so, hopefully, I will be gainfully employed very soon. I am working with my friend, Hendrix, who is a great headhunter. Let me know if you would like to connect with him for your job search."

"No, I'm good," Colbie responded. "But thank you for the offer. I have a few things in the hopper myself that I feel will be coming to fruition very soon." She suddenly perked up even more. "Before you leave, I want to give you something."

Colbie ran into the house. She was gone for almost ten minutes. When she reappeared, she had a card in her hand. She handed it to me and said, "In case you change your mind. Also, here is a book you should read. It will help to explain energy and how it works within you."

"Chakras?" I asked, reading the title.

"Yes. Understand this, and it can help explain why you feel or do what you do. Living spiritually is not all rainbows and unicorns. It takes focus, and understanding your energy can help you through the difficult patches."

***

On my drive home, Colbie's words ran through my head. Could I really make a living painting? Who was I kidding? I liked my lifestyle and didn't want to have to scrimp and penny pinch just to get by.

I placed the business card in the glove compartment and said to myself, "When I get home, I will look at the jobs that Hendrix sent over and get the ball rolling."

Just before I turned into my neighborhood, I treated myself by stopping by my favorite poke place to grab a bowl. While in line to order, I looked at the jobs that Hendrix had sent—Senior Marketing Executive for a software company and a Sales Manager for a local energy company. Not what I was hoping for, but they might have potential.

I was one person away from ordering when my phone rang.

"Hey, Hendrix," I greeted. "Can you give me a few minutes? I am just about to place an order."

"Sure."

I turned toward the server at the counter. "Yes, may I have a number four?" I followed the server down the line as he made my bowl. "Small, white rice, tuna and salmon, light on the wasabi shoyu, extra seaweed salad, tofu, and roe, with mango, ginger, and tempura flakes."

"Would you like soup?" he asked.

"Yes, and this is to-go," I responded.

He asked if I had a rewards number, and I punched it in. It said I got two dollars off my bowl. *Every little bit helps.*

I slid my card and left a two dollar tip.

"Thanks," he told me.

Nodding at the man, I asked into the phone, "Hendrix, you still there?"

"Yup. Sounds like a great bowl," he commented.

"Yeah, it's really good. Felt like treating myself today."

"I hear you on that. I love treating myself," he said then got into why he was calling. "So, I wanted to call you immediately about this opportunity. It sounds like it's right up your alley."

As Hendrix started his pitch, I got into the car and put the phone on speaker. All I heard was one hundred and seventy-five K starting salary, bonus, work from home two to three days a week, with an expense account.

"Hendrix, what is the company?" I blurted, interrupting him.

"I can't tell you who it is yet, but what I can say is that it is a really well-known Fortune 100 company, and it is a Senior Executive Sales position."

"OMG! It sounds incredible," I exclaimed.

I could tell Hendrix was smiling as he said, "Good, I thought you would say that. I will send you the information via text. Call me tomorrow so we can set up some time with the hiring manager."

"Thank you, Hendrix! You are a lifesaver."

When we hung up, I did a little car dance. I was feeling so good that I turned on the radio, opened the sunroof, and started singing at the top of my lungs. I guessed I was too into my music to see the police car on the side of the road. Next thing I knew, I heard a siren and looked in my rearview mirror as he motioned for me to pull over.

"Shit! Like I need this," I said to myself.

The officer came up on the driver's side. "Ma'am, can I see your license and registration?"

As I fumbled to put on my mask, I stammered, "I-is there something wrong?"

"You were driving thirty-five in a twenty-five mile per hour zone."

I reached over and grabbed my bag to get my license. Then I dug into the glove compartment to pull out my registration before handing both to the officer.

As he walked back to his car, I noticed the card that Colbie had given me had fallen onto the floor. I waited to pick it up, not wanting to make any sudden movement that would seem suspicious.

The officer came back about ten minutes later with a ticket, telling me to be more mindful of my speed.

I looked at the ticket. Good thing I had my mask on, as I was mouthing some choice words.

"One hundred and fifty dollars? *Ugh*."

I waited for the officer to pull away then reached over to put my registration back in the glove compartment. I picked up the business card that Colbie had given me and put it in my bag, along with my license. Then I slowly pulled out and headed home.

***

Well, that was a real bummer, I thought to myself as I walked into the house. Like I needed another bill. I hoped this didn't raise my insurance rates.

I put my dinner on the kitchen table, grabbed a can of seltzer, and then sat down to enjoy my bowl. "Good, the soup is still hot," I remarked.

As I enjoyed my meal, I thought about the job that Hendrix had mentioned. Wow, that kind of a salary, at that level, was going to mean a lot of work. I had to admit that I had been enjoying a more leisurely lifestyle since my layoff.

"*I wonder if I will be able to get back to that pace again*," I contemplated.

I finished my bowl then decided to meditate for a little while. I smiled when I thought about how far I had come with my meditation practice. My mind still wandered at times, but I found that I could get into a good space and quiet my mind much easier than before, and my foot didn't fall asleep anymore.

Halfway through my meditation, I heard, *"An opportunity is coming. Stay open."*

I finished my meditation with a smile. *Yes, I know it's my new job*, I thought to myself.

As I was getting up from my meditation, my phone rang.

"Hello?" I answered.

"Hey, Evie, it's Colbie."

"Hey, what's up?"

"Don't be mad at me," she pleaded, "but I just couldn't help myself."

"Okay ...?" I replied hesitantly.

"I took a picture of the painting you gave me and sent it to my friend, Tatum, the one who owns the consulting business helping artists." She paused. "Now, don't yell."

"I'm not going to yell, but I already told you I only do this for fun."

"Hear me out," she said. "Tatum said that she thought the painting was fabulous and that she would love to see more of your work. She has a client that loves this style and has paid exceptionally good money in the past for these types of paintings. I told her that I would ask you to call her so you can chat. She really is a lovely person, who I have known for an awfully long time. I understand if you don't want to, and I will let her know, but I have never taken such liberties before. It just felt right to do."

"Colbie, your timing is crazy." I laughed. "I just finished my meditation, and I heard that an opportunity was coming my way and to stay open. I thought it was a new job opportunity. I didn't think it would be something like this." I closed my eyes and breathed then told Colbie, "I will call your friend."

"What? You will?" Colbie screamed.

"Yes, I will."

"Do you still have the card?" she hoped.

"Funny, I was just looking at it a few minutes ago."

"I don't want to pry, but if you are so inclined, I would love to hear how the conversation goes."

"Of course, I will let you know. Thank you," I told Colbie. "Thank you for thinking of me and taking this chance. I really appreciate you!"

"Aw ... I always try to go with my feelings, and it just felt right."

I heard a crash in the background and kids yelling.

"Evie, I gotta go," Colbie exclaimed.

"No worries," I told her.

"Bye." She then hung up.

I sat back down on the floor and leaned against the wall. *Is this the opportunity?* I wondered.

Walking back out to the living room where my first painting was, I stared at it again. *This really is some of my best work. But, can I do this again and again, or was it a fluke?*

My phone rang, jerking me out of my daydream. What was it with the phone today? I never got this many calls in a day.

I looked and saw it was Reva.

"Hey, Reva," I answered.

"Thank you for answering your phone. I guess my threat worked last time," she quipped.

"Yes, it worked," I replied with a laugh. "And your timing is great."

"Why? What's up?"

"I have been presented with an opportunity."

"Great. A new job?"

"Sort of," I hedged.

"What do you mean, *sort of?*" she questioned. "Either you get paid or not."

"Yes, I *could* get paid, but ..." I trailed off.

"But what?"

"Do you remember, back in college, when I use to paint?"

"Yes."

"Well, I have taken it up again lately, and now someone may be interested in working with me to sell my paintings."

"Seriously? That is brilliant! How did this happen?"

I proceeded to give Reva the short version of my meeting with Colbie, the painting, and the speeding ticket.

Reva laughed.

"Why are you laughing?" I complained.

"Most people would look at your situation and say that it is serendipitous, but I know differently. You have just created something amazing," she explained.

"What do you mean, *created*?"

"When you have a high vibration or positive energy about something or someone, you can actually make things happen that you desire," she explained. "Down deep, you may not know it, or you don't want to admit it, but you would love to be able to paint full-time. When you think about it, your energy is more positive, and it fills you with joy. You have just manifested an amazing opportunity. I hope you stay open and allow it to fully happen."

"Well, I don't know about all that stuff, but I did agree to call her," I told her.

"Good. When?"

"I don't know ... Tomorrow?"

"Why wait? Does it feel good thinking about this opportunity? Do you have excitement?"

"Yes."

"Well then, call her now and call me afterward. Bye." With that, she hung up.

I looked at my phone. Seven p.m. It wasn't too late to call now. Well, I guessed I could leave her a message at least.

I dialed her number, my heart pounding in my chest. Then I heard, *"Hello, this is Tatum. I am sorry that I missed your call. Please leave a message at the tone."* Beep.

"Hi, Tatum. My name is Evie, a friend of Colbie's. She sent you a picture of my painting, and I was just calling to, um ... chat?" Before I could finish my message, I saw that I had an incoming call. I picked up and said, "Hello?"

"Evie, this is Tatum. Sorry I missed your call."

"Oh, wow," I said. "Thanks for calling me back so quickly. Actually, I didn't get to finish my message."

"Colbie said that you would be calling, so I picked up your call, even though I didn't recognize the number," she explained.

I smiled inside. "Oh, okay."

"So, how long have you been painting?" Tatum jumped right in.

"Well, I did a lot of painting when I was in college, but I stopped to find a real job. I just started painting again this past month," I explained.

"Interesting. I would never have guessed that you hadn't been painting regularly in years. Do you have other paintings you can show me?"

"I do have one other that I am particularly fond of."

"Just one?"

"Yes, my older paintings were done in a different mindset that doesn't emphasize where I am now in my life," I explained.

She paused. "Hmm ... well, if we do work together, I would like to see some of your other paintings, as my clientele have quite different tastes. Evie, I don't like to beat around the bush, particularly when I see something that I really like. I would love to work with you and help you sell your paintings, if you are interested. As Colbie may have explained, my clientele is from all over the world. I sell paintings to high-end hotels, office buildings, and private collectors. I have one who would love the barn painting, so I would assume that they would like your other piece, as well."

My heart was racing, and I was trying to control my breathing, as to not give away my excitement. "Tatum, this sounds very interesting, but I lived the life of a starving artist, and I don't want to go back there."

"If you can produce more paintings like this, I would highly doubt that you would be classified as a *starving artist*," she proclaimed. "My commission is fifteen percent. I can send over the paperwork that outlines my standard agreement. Send me pictures of your other painting, and I will give you a ballpark of what I believe it could sell for."

"Wow, okay. I will take some pictures tonight, then, and send them right over. Thank you, and I look forward to learning more," I told her, trying not to squeal with excitement.

"Great. I look forward to seeing more of your work. And Evie"—she paused—"I noticed you said that you stopped to get a real job. If this is where your passion lies, and you have fun doing it, this can definitely be a real job for you. You just have to own it. Have a wonderful evening."

I hung up the phone and sat there in pure amazement. *Someone would actually be interested in buying my painting? This is unbelievable.* I had to call Reva.

Reva picked up on the first ring and said, "So, what happened? Tell me every little detail."

I told Reva everything, still in total disbelief. Then I realized that I needed to take photos of my other painting to send to Tatum, so I cut the call short, telling her that I would call her tomorrow and let her know what happened.

"Evie, before you go, I just want you to know how proud I am of you. Believe in yourself, because you truly are amazing. I love ya. Goodnight."

I put the phone down, and this wave of emotion washed over me. It was a combination of joy, pride, fear, and excitement all rolled up into one messy emotion. I fell onto the couch and just started to cry. It was the most incredible cry that I'd had in a long time. Then I wiped my face, got up, and started taking pictures of my painting.

***

I took about half a dozen pictures, trying to get the right light. Then I finally decided on two pictures and sent them to Tatum. Afterward, I jumped into the shower, needing to relax. There were so many emotions flowing through me that I was all wound up.

Could I really do this? I had created two paintings; who was to say that I could paint more? What if they didn't sell? Could I have a full-time job and still paint? I had the opportunity for a great paying job, just as I had asked. Did I go for that or paint?

The questions were swirling around, and my emotions went from excited to straight-up fear. As more and more questions started popping up in my mind, I was filled with doubt. Then my thoughts turned from, *can I?* to *I can't*. I felt awful.

Who was I kidding? I couldn't do this. I needed to listen to my grandfather. It was time to grow up and get a real job, to stick with what I knew. I had proven myself there, so why should I try doing something new, especially at my age?

I crawled into bed and just stared at the ceiling. With all of these thoughts going through my head, there was no way I was going to fall asleep, so I sat up and started to meditate. I just needed to breathe and try to quiet my mind.

As soon as I was able to slow my thoughts down, one word popped into my head.

Ego.

All of a sudden, I remembered the conversation that Colbie and I'd had. That ego was there to limit me, and it didn't play fair. Boy, was she right. But she had also said that ego was there to protect me, which made me wonder if I was heading toward making a big mistake. How was I supposed to know what was ego and what was my heart?

I opened my eyes, totally confused. What was I supposed to do?

I started feeling really tired, but before I lay down, I said out loud, "Higher self, please give me clarity." Then I turned off the light and fell asleep.

In the middle of the night, I heard, *"Ego is doubt. If it feels good, it is your heart."*

***

Doubt is ego. Feels good is heart. So, I guessed I did get an answer if asked. Knowing that made me feel more comfortable, but I still found it hard to just shut ego down.

Today felt different, like something was coming, so I got myself motivated, made breakfast, and got dressed. I sent Hendrix a text, asking when he had time to meet today to discuss the job. He responded that he would call me around ten. Great, that gave me some time to get my thoughts straight.

As I was enjoying my coffee and scrolling through social media, an email came in from Tatum. It contained the agreement and what she believed I should sell my painting for. After seeing the price, I dropped the phone on the floor. Then, as I searched for my phone, I smacked my head on the table. *Ouch!* It was as if my higher self was smacking me upside the head to say, "*See? I told you so.*" Who knew my higher self had such humor? Personally, I thought Reva had something to do with it.

I smiled as I grabbed my phone.

I went through the email again. *Holy Toledo!* Tatum believed I could sell my painting for three thousand dollars. I felt a huge smile come across my face. Who knew this could feel so good? In my entire painting career, I didn't think I had even made three thousand dollars.

As I basked in excitement, Hendrix called me.

"Good morning, Evie. How are you doing?"

"Morning, Hendrix. I am doing great."

"Glad to hear it. Why so good?" he asked.

I gave him a rundown of what had happened and truly felt that he was as excited about the news as I was.

"That is amazing news! Are you going to sell your work?"

"I think so," I admitted.

"So, is this a part-time gig or are you going to take the leap and do it full-time?"

"I don't know … I really don't know what to do," I whined.

"Are you excited about being a full-time painter?"

"Yes," I sheepishly responded.

"Why are you so shy about this, Evie? This is your true self. Why do you want to continue to live a lie … just for money?"

"Money *is* kind of important," I pointed out.

"Yes, I know, but so is your happiness. So, what are we doing here? Are we talking about the job opportunity, or are we talking about a new life?" he questioned.

I paused for a long moment then told him, "I would still like to move forward with an interview."

"Okay, we can do that. But, Evie, I want to share a few lessons that I learned a long time ago: there is never a wrong answer, opportunities always come, and don't let fear, or ego, make your decision for you."

"Wait—what do you mean that there is never a wrong answer?" I repeated.

"We are put on this Earth to experience life in its fullest. That means all experiences. If you choose to move forward with painting, enjoy that experience. If you get this job, enjoy that experience. If you decide that painting isn't for you, what's to stop you from doing something else? That also applies to this job opportunity. You have free will. There are always new and different opportunities. You create your life, whether you know it or not. Once you know that, it makes things so much easier, and your higher self is right there with you. Think of it this way: you create your life through your desires. You state your desire and you put positive, focused energy toward it. Then your higher self acts as your GPS, guiding you so that your desires come to fruition or manifest," Hendrix explains.

"Really? That sounds kind of easy."

"Really. But there will be times when it doesn't seem as easy. It all comes down to knowing that *you* are in control. *You* are creating your life every day. This is a double-edged sword. You manifest what you focus on with emotion and energy. It can be what you want or what you don't want. So, be mindful of what you think about. Also, ego plays a big role, and it takes time and focus to quiet ego, but it can be done. Know you can do it. Trust in yourself."

"Hendrix, what would I do without you? You have truly been a life saver."

"Aw ... shucks, you make me blush. Okay, enough of the love fest, let's get an interview scheduled for you. How does Friday at eleven sound? Video call," he added.

"Sure, that will work."

"Okay, I will send the meeting details by this afternoon. I have already sent over your resume, and I believe that they have checked out your online profile. You will be meeting with the HR department first. Then, if things go well, the hiring manager. If they want you, I assume this could all get tied up with a bow by next Friday. Sound good?"

I didn't respond immediately.

"Evie, you still there?"

"Sorry. Yes, sounds good."

"Great. I will be in touch. Have a great day and stop worrying. Live in the present, have fun, and it will all work out."

When we hung up, I found myself not as excited as I thought I would be.

***

After lunch, I gave Colbie a call. She wasn't available, so I just left her a message with the news. Then I walked into the former junk room and decided I wanted to paint. If I was considering doing this for a living, I needed to see if I could paint on demand. So, I set myself up and looked at the blank canvas, trying to think of what I should paint.

Nothing came to me.

I looked out the window.

Still no inspiration.

Hmm ... maybe I should go outside to clear my head.

It was a sunny day, but there was still a bit of a chill, so I threw on my jacket and took a walk around the neighborhood. I felt like I was looking at everything but seeing nothing. I started to feel a little panicked that I had no inspiration. When I used to paint in college, I could find anything to paint. Now I was walking around, feeling like I was blind.

In my panic, I felt the compulsion to run.

Please know that running was not my strong suit, but I just had to get away. It felt like anxiety was chasing me, and I just had to get as far away from it as possible.

After running for what seemed like forever, and almost hyperventilating due to my mask, I stopped and buckled over, trying to catch my breath. When I stood back up, I realized that I was about two miles away from my house. In another time or place, I would have called for a car to bring me home, but now it was probably better that I walked, calming myself and taking in the fresh air.

When I finally got back to my house, I was less anxious but still concerned about my future. I grabbed a glass of water and collapsed onto the couch. I was starting to feel better when my phone rang.

"Hey, Colbie," I answered weakly.

"Evie, what's the matter? Are you okay?"

I proceed to tell her about the conversation with Tatum, the job opportunity with Hendrix, and my failed attempt at painting on demand.

"Oh, honey, be kind to yourself. You obviously were not in the right mindset to paint."

"Well, how could I have done it before? I wasn't even trying," I told her.

"That's the point; you weren't *trying* before. Tell me what you were thinking when you painted the barn picture."

"Well, I wasn't planning on painting. I heard the voice say *paint*. I argued a bit, but then it said to paint my feelings, how I felt during our meeting. Then it just happened."

Colbie sighed. "Evie, you were trying too hard. You were in your head and not your heart. When you find yourself in that place, you just need to breathe, turn off your head, and listen to your heart. What makes you feel good or brings you a lot of emotion. The best thing I can tell you is to stop looking and start feeling. If you paint your feelings, then it will come easily and naturally."

"This is all so new to me. I just don't remember having to do this last time."

"Well, that could be the difference between you being asked to sell your painting and not selling anything back in college. Feel it then paint it."

"Colbie, how do you see so clearly?"

"It doesn't always seem so clear, but when I am looking from the outside in, I can see things that you may not be able to see. I always try to be in the moment, and I tune into your energy. Plus, I also receive help from Spirit. I am guided on what to say to help you understand what is going on," she explained.

"Thank you. I will admit that I was feeling very anxious, and it seemed like I couldn't see anything. I was looking but saw nothing. I will try again, but this time with a quieter mind."

"Wonderful! And please give yourself some grace. Things take time, and you are just remembering how to do some of this stuff. Oh, and congratulations. Even if you do not end up painting or working with Tatum, just know that you are gifted. Share your gift however works best for you. We will all be better for it."

"Thank you, Colbie. Have I told you how I love talking to you? You always put me at peace. I guess that is your gift. Thank you for sharing it with me."

"You are welcome. Have a great evening." Then she hung up.

I sat there, thinking about the conversation, and decided to try painting again. I almost grabbed a glass of wine but decided against it. I would do this free and clear. I would paint my feelings.

I headed back into the junk room and stepped up to the easel. I closed my eyes and took a few deep breaths. Then I started to paint.

My strokes were frantic. It felt like I was painting like a mad woman. No rhyme or reason. I felt anxious and stressed, like when I was running through town. By the time I finished, there was paint everywhere. The drop cloth caught maybe a quarter of the paint that I was slinging around.

I stepped back and looked at the painting. It was nothing like I had ever painted before—so strong and erratic but beautiful at the same time. And now I felt so calm. It felt like I had let go of years of anxiety and stress and put it on a canvas for all to see.

I lay on the floor and let the calmness wash over me. I never had this type of emotion working in corporate America. Granted, there had been stress and elation from a big sale or a promotion, but nothing like what I had just gone through. I loved this feeling.

CHAPTER 6 — UNCHARTERED WATERS

My paint session had left me feeling so free that I took the opportunity to respond back to Tatum.

> *Tatum, thank you for the information and the suggested sale price. I am extremely interested in moving forward and would love to work with you.*
> *Attached, please find a picture of my latest work. It is titled* Frantic to Freedom. *If you have time this week, I would love to meet for coffee so we can discuss this arrangement further.*
> *Thank you for your belief in me.*
> *Evie.*

I read the note two times then hit *send*. "And away we go ..."

I went back to the former junk room and thought about how I was going to get the paint off the walls. Then I heard, *"This is your studio."*

I nodded. "Yes" I said out loud. This was my art studio.

Whoa, saying that gave me chills throughout my body.

After a shower and food, I turned on some music, as there was nothing that I wanted to watch on TV, and started walking through my house. *If I am to be a full-time artist, do I need such a big house? What do I need to make myself happy?* Two bedrooms, two bathrooms, a small yard, a kitchen, and a living room. It would be nice to have a shed that maybe I could turn into a larger studio, but that could come later. That was a significant downsizing than what I had now.

It seemed like my whole life had been working toward getting more stuff, bigger stuff, nicer stuff. Now that I had this time—being at home, jobless, living through a pandemic—I realized that it was just stuff and didn't seem as important.

I started to laugh as I realized I actually had that exact space on the Vineyard. If only I could get there. One day soon, I hoped.

***

The next day, I decided to go down to the local art store to splurge on some new supplies. I planned to get canvases, paint, and a few new brushes. I found myself excited for this excursion, so I ate, got dressed, threw a clean mask into my bag, and then headed out to the art supply store. When I got there, it was pretty quiet, and I basically had the store to myself.

As I walked around, a young, heavily-tattooed woman walked up to me named Shiloh.

"Do you need help finding anything?" she asked.

"Hi, Shiloh," I greeted her, and she looked at me with a shocked expression, seeming to be surprised that I knew her name. I pointed to her name tag, and she blushed.

She recovered and asked again, "How can I help you?"

"I am looking for some canvases, brushes, and oil paint."

She brought me to each section, and we started talking shop.

"So, what medium do you work in?" I probed. I could tell that she was an artist, too, by her wording.

"I work in all mediums, but right now, I am really feeling watercolors. They are so beautiful and can be so soft but are truly the hardest thing I have ever worked in."

"Shiloh, can I ask how you get over the fear that people will not like your paintings, or that they won't sell?" Since we were really the only two in the store, I felt comfortable asking her some more personal questions.

"Hmm ... yes, that is a hard one. What I do is remind myself that I am painting for *me*, and if people don't like what I am painting, it is their issue, not mine. If worse comes to worse, I keep my paintings and just enjoy them myself. I believe there will always be someone who appreciates what you do. It may not be a lot of people, it may not be while you are alive, or you may never know who it is, but there is at least one person. So, just do what you love and know that there is someone out there who likes what you are doing."

I smiled. That was pretty sound advice from someone so young.

She helped me carry all my items to the check out and rang me up. "That will be two hundred, thirty-five dollars, and eighteen cents," she said with a slight cringe.

I laughed. "Well, I better sell my paintings. Thanks for the help and guidance."

She smiled and gave me a wave goodbye.

As I put my things in the trunk, I heard, "Evie, is that you?"

I looked over and saw Hendrix in his car. Wow, I had forgotten how handsome he was. Seemed like all I did was text or talk to him over the phone. It felt like ages since I had last seen him.

I gave a coy smile. "What are you doing here?"

"I love the coffee shop over there. Here to get my morning brew. And, what are you doing?"

"Picking up some painting supplies," I responded proudly.

"Good to hear. Can I buy you a cup of coffee?" he offered.

"Sure." I thought to myself how nice it would be to have some human interaction, and the fact that it was with Hendrix was a plus.

He smiled. "Meet you over there."

I put the rest of the stuff in my car then walked over to the coffee shop.

When we walked in, I ordered a decaf and he asked for a green tea.

He looked at me. "Decaf?"

"Yes, I realized at the beginning of this journey that too much caffeine is not my friend."

We grabbed our drinks then moved to sit outside.

"So, you are painting more?" he started the conversation.

I blushed. "I actually finished another painting last night."

He grinned. "So, can I officially say that I have a friend who is an artist?"

"I don't know if I would go that far," I scoffed with a laugh.

"Why not?"

I simply shrugged.

"Evie, declare it, believe it, and it will be," he coached. "If you don't believe it, then who else is going to?"

Hendrix raised a good point. I thought about it then said, "I hear you." Then I smiled. "Yes, you can say you have a friend who is an artist."

He nodded, still smiling, then went into professional, his tone changing. "So, I confirmed your interview for Friday. When I get back home, I will send you the details."

He had caught me in mid-drink, and I almost choked on my coffee.

"Evie, are you okay?"

"Yes," I sputtered between coughs. *That was weird*, I thought to myself.

My face turned beet red after I realized that I had coughed all over Hendrix. Not the impression I wanted to leave him with.

We talked a little longer then said our goodbyes, giving each other a hug. I had to admit that it was a wonderful hug, big and warm. I used to take hugs for granted. Seemed like they were no different than a handshake. We would do it as a greeting and as a goodbye. But now, they seemed to mean so much more. I didn't know if it was the time we were in, the people I hugged, or how I looked at life now. No matter what it was, that was a damn good hug.

When I got home, I put everything in my studio then checked my email. Both Tatum and Hendrix had sent me something. I opened Tatum's email first.

> *Evie,*
>
> *I am so happy to hear that we will be working together. I genuinely believe you are exceptionally talented and that your art will sell. I would love to meet for coffee to sign the agreement and talk about next steps.*
>
> *Also, your newest piece is to die for! The frustration and anxiety just leaps off the canvas. I am sure that I can also find a buyer for that piece, as well.*
>
> *Let's shoot for Friday around 2:00 to meet. There is this great little coffee shop in the Blue Hills shopping area. You may know it. It is next to the art supply store. Let me know if that time works for you. And please bring both paintings so I can see them in person.*
>
> *Thank you and have a great day.*

Funny, I guessed there was something about that coffee shop.

Hendrix's email provided the video call information for Friday's interview, the HR representative's information, and an overview of the company. I opened the attachment that had the company overview.

"Rhode Marketing," I said out loud. *Holy shit!* I hadn't known that I was interviewing with them. It was a highly reputable firm that worked all over the world. The position was for their new environmental division, leading a team of twenty-five people from across the globe.

Wow, I thought to myself. *This is an amazing opportunity.*

Just then, I felt tremendous anxiety. If I got this job, I was sure I wouldn't have time to paint, but I couldn't give it up now that I had rediscovered it. I loved it too much.

My mind started to go into a tailspin. Back and forth. Pros and cons. I knew I needed to slow my mind down, but I just couldn't seem able to.

I grabbed my phone and called Reva. The phone rang and rang, and my anxiety grew at the thought of not being able to speak to her. My breathing started to become quicker and shorter. Finally, she picked up.

"Reva!" I almost yelled. "I need your help!"

"What is it? What's wrong?"

In my calmest voice, I tried to tell her what was going on. Needless to say, it was not calm and, at this point, I was fighting back tears.

Then I heard loud and clear, "Evie, shut up and breathe. *Breathe.* Keep on breathing. Big, deep inhales and full exhales. Breathe, breathe."

Finally, I started to calm myself. I wiped at my face and closed my eyes.

"Reva, I am so sorry," I told her then started to cry again.

"For what?" she snapped.

"Sorry that you had to see that full-on freak-out. I'm usually never like this, but my emotions have been on a real rollercoaster lately."

"Please, Evie," she scoffed. "Remember, we went to college together. I have seen you in worse places than this. Remember that time when you were drunk and needed to sing from the mountaintops in your underwear because you were in love with your English Lit professor?"

I laughed. I had been such a hopeless romantic back then. Reva had done everything she could to talk me out of that situation, but it hadn't worked. Next thing I knew, she had been pulling me out of a tree, because that had been the closest thing we had to a mountain.

As she continued the story, I told her, "Shut up," and started laughing hysterically. Reva always knew how to handle me.

"Now that you're back, want to tell me what is really going on?" she invited.

I proceeded to tell her more clearly that I didn't know what to do. I had this great opportunity with the marketing firm, and I also had my love of painting. I was afraid that I couldn't do both, but I didn't know if I even wanted to do both.

Finally, I blurted out, "I'm scared."

"Why wouldn't you be?" she noted. "You are in unchartered waters. But guess what? You don't know what the future holds, so why worry about it? Worrying about tomorrow takes away today's peace. Stay in the present and enjoy the ride. Enjoy the fact that you are interviewing with an amazing company for an equally amazing job. You can also enjoy that you are an artist doing what you love and will finally be selling your paintings. Be in the here and now. When you try to figure out the future, that is when the anxiety sets in. All you can control is how you act *now*. Focus on clarity when you need to make your decisions. You may find out, after your interview, that the job just isn't for you. Or maybe that you could still paint *and* have the job. You don't know until you know."

"Okay, okay. I hear you," I said.

"Evie, leave me and go meditate. Ask for guidance, and it will be given. Call me later so I know that you are all right."

"Okay, will do. Thank you, Reva."

"Anytime, kiddo. Love ya," she stated then hung up.

I put the phone down and closed my eyes. I took some deep breaths to calm my mind. A few minutes later, I said, "Higher self, I need guidance. I don't know what to do. Please help."

I then heard, *"Trust your heart. You will feel what is right. Trust it and allow it to happen."*

***

When Friday arrived, I woke up early and lay in bed, giving my appreciation to my higher self to guide me in the right decision. Then I made a really good breakfast—an omelet with spinach, tomato, and feta—wheat toast, water, and a big cup of decaf coffee, and I stayed away from all social media to keep my head clear and to be in the moment.

After breakfast, I showered, did some stretching, and looked in my closet for my interview outfit. Well, at least the top part. Today, I felt bright yet sophisticated, so I picked a floral, silk bow blouse with simple gold hoop earrings. I wore my hair tied back with clean, simple makeup. I checked myself in the mirror at least ten times before I logged into my computer. Then I checked my makeup one last time before I joined the call.

I was the first one on the call, so I kept myself calm by mindfully breathing. Nothing too deep, just in case the HR person came on and I was in mid-inhale or exhale. At eleven on the dot, Rhode's HR representative opened the call.

"Good morning, Ms. Prince. My name is Simone Bragg. Nice to meet you," he greeted. Simone Bragg was a middle-aged, well-dressed man with piercing blue-green eyes. He seemed generally uninterested but was putting on a smile to be polite.

"Good morning," I replied. "And please, call me Evie."

"Wonderful. Well, we were extremely interested to see your resume come across our desk for this Senior Executive Marketing/Sales position for our new environmental group. You have a lot of experience that we are looking for. I believe Hendrix provided you with an overview of the position?"

"Yes, he did, thank you."

"Great. We are looking for someone who can create this team from the ground up. We have a handful of inside candidates that we feel would be great for this group, but we would leave it up to the right candidate to do all the hiring for the team. That would include the international roles, as well. This is really a blue-sky type of position, so the right candidate will be required to do approximately thirty to forty percent travel to meet with potential candidates, and then, once hired, provide onboarding for the roles and ongoing management. Does this sound like something that you would be qualified to do?" he questioned.

"Yes, I do feel that I am qualified to hire the right team. I have done this type of larger scale hiring in my past roles, and I feel confident that I would hire the right highly skilled people to fill the necessary positions."

"Excellent. Since this is a new division, the right candidate will be required to be a jack of all trades—budgeting, working with vendors across all disciplines, producing marketing materials, and of course meeting sales goals. I know this is a diversified role. Do you feel that you would be up for the challenge?"

I smiled and somewhat laughed. "Mr. Bragg, this definitely is a diversified role, and I am happy to say that, over my tenure at other firms, I have excelled in all of these roles separately and collectively. And yes, I believe I am up for the challenge."

"Perfect. Do you have any questions for me?" he inquired.

"Yes, I do. I understand that I will be responsible for the creation, support, and management of this team, but will there be any support from other internal Rhode Marketing teams, or will we be considered somewhat of a separate entity?"

"For the time being, you could consider your team a separate entity and, based upon the team's success, it would determine how the rest of the Rhode organization will support. Does that answer your question?"

"Yes, perfectly."

"Wonderful. Well, if you have no further questions, thank you for your time, and we will be in touch via Hendrix regarding any next steps."

"Mr. Bragg, let me just say that I appreciate the opportunity and your consideration. Thank you and have a great day."

We both smiled at each other then signed off.

Well, that was as pleasant as a kick in the butt. I hoped Mr. Bragg was not representing the rest of the organization.

I turned off my computer then changed clothes, putting on some comfortable jeans and a simple but colorful sweater. I then made myself some lunch and decompressed on the couch.

That conversation had really taken a lot out of me. It had made me feel like I was an actor playing my former self. The discussion had felt so impersonal, like he didn't really care who I was, that he was just checking a box and moving on to the next person.

I gave Hendrix a ring.

"So, how did it go?"

"Good, I think."

"What do you mean, *you think*? Were you qualified?" he asked with a smile in his voice.

"Yes. Of course I was qualified, but there was just something that didn't sit well with me. I can't put my finger on it."

"All right. Well, now we wait. As I mentioned, they want to have this process closed out by next Friday, so I would assume that I will hear from them no later than Tuesday or Wednesday regarding next steps," he explained.

"Yup, that sounds good. I am focused on living in the present, so what happens will happen."

"Huh? Who are you? Who took my Evie?" Hendrix jested.

"Very funny. I actually had a panic attack earlier this week, and I don't ever want to go through that again. A good friend of mine reminded me that, if I want to remove anxiety, that I should live in the present. I cannot predict the future; all I can do is focus on what I want and be."

"Wow. This is a whole new Evie. I likie. Not that I didn't like the old Evie, but you seem to have a new confidence about you, like you know everything will work out."

I shrugged, though he couldn't see it. "Well, I have had some fantastic teachers, present company included, and I finally understand that I *do* have control. I *can* create my own life."

"Good on ya, Evie. I am so happy and proud of you. I know whatever happens, you will make the right decision for who you truly are," he told me.

"Thank you, Hendrix. I gotta run to another appointment."

"Cool. I will call you next week."

Hanging up the phone, I grabbed my paintings, my bag, and a mask, and then I headed to the car.

As I walked down the stairs, Sue, my neighbor, was on her front porch.

"Beautiful paintings," she commented.

I smiled. "Thank you."

***

I arrived at the coffee shop a few minutes early, so I grabbed a table and waited. The day had warmed up nicely, so I enjoyed the sun.

I had just closed my eyes to truly feel the moment when I heard, "Evie?"

I opened my eyes to see a tall, slender woman looking at me. Her black hair was cut in a short pixie, and she had a welcoming smile.

I stood up. "Tatum, so nice to meet you."

Tatum offered to grab us some coffee then returned within a few minutes. For a moment, she just looked at me. It made me feel a little awkward, but I went with it. Finally, she said, "Colbie said you have a wonderful energy."

I paused then said, "Thank you."

She smiled then went into business mode. "So, before we get to the business side of things, tell me about you."

I started to give her the rundown of my last job, etcetera, when she stopped me mid-sentence.

"No. I want to learn about *you*. Who are you?" she probed.

"Oh," I said, a little taken aback. I had never been asked that type of question. I tried to answer but didn't know how and fumbled with my words.

"Okay, let's try this again," she said. "I will tell you about me, and then we can go from there. I am an entrepreneur who works with beautiful things and interesting people. I have a husband, two kids, and two dogs. I love the ocean, meditating, having interesting conversations, and I believe that we can create amazing things, if we choose to."

I thought to myself, *Shit, how am I going to follow that?* Then I replied, "I am a single, forty-one-year-old woman who is on a journey of discovery."

"Wonderful to meet you." She smiled. "But I noticed that you did not say that you were an artist. Why is that?"

"Umm ... I don't know."

"Do you believe that you are an artist, a painter?" she inquired.

"Yes, I believe so."

"Then, why don't you say it? Speak your truth."

I blushed a bit then took a deep breath and said, "I am an artist who is on a journey of discovery."

"There we go! Very nice to meet you, Evie."

We proceeded to have a fascinating conversation about life, how we had both gotten to where we were now, and how she conducted her business. Everything she said to me resonated. She listened intently to what I had to say and was completely in the moment with me. I loved how she was so transparent, honest, and genuinely wanted to create and share beautiful things. She believed it was her gift to help people communicate their truth and art was one of the most beautiful ways of doing it.

After an hour of talking and laughing, we started to talk business. I showed her my work, and she pulled up her sleeve to show me the goosebumps on her arm. She suggested that we price the first painting at three thousand dollars and the second at twenty-five hundred.

"Evie, these paintings are absolutely amazing. I have two buyers in mind that I would like to contact immediately. I will stand firm with these prices, as sometimes these buyers like to haggle. If, for whatever reason, I feel that they will really walk due to the price, I will contact you, and we can discuss further. Does that work for you?"

"Yes, that sounds fine to me." I signed the agreement, and instead of shaking hands, she stood up and gave me a hug. It was one of those wonderful hugs, long and warm.

"Thank you, Evie, for trusting me to represent you and your work. I am honored to know you and to work with you," she said.

On the drive home, I gave Colbie a call.

"Well, I did it," I told her.

"Did what?"

"I am officially a represented artist. I am working with Tatum."

"That is absolutely amazing! I am so happy for you. How do you feel?"

"I feel fantastic, and the whole process just felt right," I answered. "She is an awesome person. I felt like I have known her my entire life. She really gets to the heart of the matter, but in a loving way."

"Evie, I can feel that things are really starting to open up for you. Ride it. Think of yourself as a leaf in a stream. The leaf does not go upstream; it just goes where the water takes it. If there is a rock, the leaf just glides around it. Life can be that easy if you just let it go and follow your heart."

"How is that you always know what to say to me? I probably should tell you that I also had an interview with Rhode Marketing for a Senior Executive Sales position this morning."

"What? Rhode Marketing? How did you get *that* interview?" she wondered.

"My headhunter friend made it happen."

"And ...?"

"And ..." I mock-teased, "I wasn't feeling it. I met with the HR representative. It was so impersonal. This is a build-from-the-ground-up kind of position. It pays, but I would be spending every waking minute working. If they want to move forward, I will meet with the hiring manager next week. They are looking to have everything tied up by next Friday."

"Hmm … not up for the challenge?" she joked.

I paused to think. "No, more like, I don't want this challenge. I want to create beauty."

"You already do."

"Yes, but I want to create beauty as my job."

I heard Colbie clapping. "Congratulations, Evie."

"For what?"

"For making a decision. Now, are you going to take the leap of faith?"

"I don't think I have another option. I finally know what makes me happy, and I definitely know what does not make me happy. I choose happy."

"Then keep that feeling close to your heart always and make all of your decisions with that as the purpose. Some may not understand, but it doesn't matter. *You* know what you are doing," Colbie advised.

Her words were like a big hug.

"Thank you. I will."

CHAPTER 7 — PURGE

Why did I have so many pairs of shoes? I looked at all the boxes and noticed I didn't wear half of them. Then I started flipping through my clothes and quickly came to the same realization—I had way too many. I spent all of Saturday cleaning out. I went through my closet and removed more than half my clothes, like the items that I had thought I would wear or the result of a retail therapy session. The more I purged, the more I wanted to get rid of things.

As I went through my house, I asked myself if I really needed this item or that item. If I had to think about it, then I did not need it. Now that I had remembered what made me happy, I focused on bringing that into my entire life, and purging allowed me to get rid of the old to bring in the new.

Since things were opening up, I decided to have a garage sale on Sunday. By Saturday afternoon, I walked around the neighborhood and hung signs, announcing the garage sale. I knew it was late notice, but I also knew that I would get visitors. I priced each item of clothing, no matter what style, new or used, at five dollars. Some items still had their tags on them so people would know what a great deal they were getting. All shoes were priced at two dollars a pair, and household items went for one dollar. I did have a few larger items, like a dresser and matching bedside tables, that were specially priced, but ninety-nine percent of the items were five dollars and under.

By seven thirty on Sunday morning, I had my first customer, and then there was a steady stream of people throughout the morning. Everyone was doing what they were supposed to—wearing masks, keeping socially distant. All I heard was people saying, "Really? This is only five dollars?" or "Two dollars? For real?" For some reason, hearing that gave me real joy.

Susan came out and walked around, too.

"Evie, are you planning on moving?" she speculated.

"No, just felt the need to clean out. You should try it. It feels really good," I revealed.

She gave me a once-over. "You look really different. Younger. What have you been doing?"

"Oh, just creating the life that I want to live," I answered with a smile.

"You weren't living the life you wanted before? But you were so successful."

"I was successful, but I wasn't happy. I remembered what makes me happy, and I am sticking to it."

"Okay," she said, looking me up and down again then walking away.

I smiled, knowing she did not understand.

Normally, I would have felt the need to explain myself, but I knew what I was doing now, and it felt so good.

By eleven a.m., just about everything was gone. There was only the dresser, the bedside tables, and a few clothing items left.

A car pulled up, and I recognized the woman getting out of the car. It was the young lady who had taken my office chair.

"Hi again. Do you remember me?" she asked.

"Yes. Triniti, isn't it? How are you?" I asked. I remembered her because that had been the first time that I had learned about true intuition.

"You remember! I'm great. I had a funny feeling again that I needed to swing by here. Seems like I missed the party."

"There are a few items left, but yes, a majority of it is gone. Is the office chair working well for you?"

"Yes, it is perfect." She beamed then explained, "I am just getting back on my feet again after a bad relationship. I just got this new job, and I didn't have the extra cash to get a desk chair. So, you really helped me out a lot." She looked around, and I saw her eyes lock onto the dresser. "Ooo ... that is a beautiful dresser," she complimented.

"Thanks. They have matching bedside tables to go with it."

"Wow, do I dare ask how much? They are gorgeous."

"How much do you have?"

"Umm ..." She looked into her wallet. "I have thirty dollars."

"Well, it is your lucky day. I am only asking fifteen for the set."

"*What?* Are you kidding me?" she screamed.

"Nope, I am not kidding, but you have to get a truck to take them away."

"I have a friend who has a truck. We can come back here in about an hour. Is that okay?"

"That would be perfect," I told her.

Triniti handed over the fifteen dollars with a smile. Then she grabbed me and gave me one of those wonderful hugs, big and warm, and whispered in my ear, "You don't know how thankful I am for you. You are a beautiful light." That said, she let go then ran to her car to call her friend.

Triniti rolled down her window before driving off and said, "We will be back in an hour. Thank you for everything."

I waved. "Okay."

I grabbed the remaining items and started putting them into my car to bring over to the donation center.

As I was cleaning up, Susan came over again.

"I saw what you did," she said, "and it was beautiful."

"I did what made me feel happy." I shrugged. "I think I got more out of it than she did."

Susan gave me a funny look then looked around. "Do you need any help cleaning up?"

"No, but thank you for asking."

As I cleaned, I could feel Susan looking at me.

"Evie, there is something really different about you. You exude happiness. Can you tell me how I can be that happy?" she requested.

"Sure, listen to your heart."

"Huh? Listen to my heart?"

"Yes. It will tell you everything you need to know."

She gave me an unsure smile and mumbled, "Thanks." Then she walked back to her house.

Just as I was putting the last of the items in the car, a truck pulled up. Triniti and her friend were all smiles as they packed up the furniture. Before they left, Triniti gave me a beautiful, hand-painted little vase.

"Thank you again," she told me. "I made this, and I want you to have it. When you put flowers in it, I hope it reminds you of the beauty you bring to this world."

As they drove off, I was so overwhelmed with joy that I cried happy tears.

I went inside to place my new vase on the kitchen windowsill so I would always see it and remember the joy of that moment. Then, sitting at the kitchen table with a yogurt, I admired my new vase. It really was beautiful.

In fact, I was so inspired by its beauty that I decided to paint. I felt like this should be a small painting that captured the feeling of the moment, the joy that both Triniti and I had felt, so I used blues, greens, and yellows. Painting this gave me as much joy as I had received when it had happened. I would not sell this one. This one was just for me.

Afterward, I took a shower then jumped into bed. I had recently started to journal, as I wanted to remember all the miraculous things that were happening to me.

Tonight, as I wrote down the activities of the day, I heard the voice say, *"Write a letter to yourself."*

I stopped and thought about it. Then I began.

> *Dearest Evie,*
> *I know that you struggle to know what to do.*
> *Your mind is strong and has gotten you far, but it*
> *is time to use your heart. Trust it; it will not lead*
> *you astray. Feel, feel, feel. You will have all that*
> *you desire. You know everything that you need to*
> *know. All you have to do is ask, and you will be*
> *answered.*
> *You are magnificent.*
> *You are powerful.*
> *You are everything, and everything is you.*
> *Trust that the heart knows best.*
> *Trust in yourself.*

After I finished, I realized that I had not written this to myself. It was more like I had dictated what I had been hearing in my head.

Who is my higher self? I wondered.

***

Lately, I had been taking long walks to get exercise, but also to get inspiration for future paintings. This morning felt a bit different. I had the urge to call Hendrix, but I didn't know why.

I dialed Hendrix's number, and it only rang a few times before he picked up.

"Good morning, Evie. Happy Monday," he answered.

"Good morning, Hendrix."

"So, what can I do for you?" he wondered.

"Um … I don't know. I just had the urge to call you."

"Well, your timing is great. I heard back from Rhode Marketing and—"

"Stop!"

"What?"

"Stop. I don't want to know," I told him.

"You don't want to know …?" He trailed off.

"I don't want to know if they want to give me a second interview."

"But … why?"

"I have made my decision. I do not want to move forward with the process. I have decided to be a full-time artist."

"Oh, Evie. Congratulations! I am so happy for you. You are taking the leap."

"I guess you can say I am. Honestly, I couldn't bring myself to willingly be unhappy again. I have found what makes me happy, and I trust in myself to make it work."

"There is that new Evie who I just love," Hendrix boasted.

"Well, I will give them a call today and let them know."

"Thank you, Hendrix. I really appreciate all the time that you have given to me, both professionally and spiritually. I'm sorry that I couldn't help you hit your numbers this month."

"Evie, I would much rather work with people to help them find their passion than just to find them a job. You did me a favor, so *I* should be thanking *you*."

"Maybe when you go out on your own, you should be a passion hunter versus a headhunter," I suggested.

"Hmm … maybe, Evie, maybe."

When we hung up, I felt so light. It was like a ton of bricks had just been removed from my shoulders. I sat there, thinking about what I had just done and realized that I was an entrepreneur now. I needed to figure out how to build my artistic career.

I decided to send Tatum an email, asking for her help.

Tatum, I have decided to move forward as a full-time artist and am looking for some guidance on how to set up and market my work. Hoping you would be interested in helping me. Do you have time this week to meet?

Let me know.
Thank you.
Evie.

Within ten minutes, I received an email from her.

> *Yippee! So excited for you! And, of course I*
> *would love to help you. Wednesday, same coffee*
> *shop. Can't wait to get to work.*

Now I needed to put my skills to the test.

I knew marketing, and I knew sales, but I had never had to market or sell myself like this before. What to do first?

I grabbed a piece of paper and sat down at the kitchen table. Then I wrote at the top:

Things to Do To Start a Successful Art Business
Paint
Brand name
Logo
Website
Social Media

Painting was ongoing, but what should my brand name be? *Evie Painting Extraordinaire?* Maybe too much. I had to laugh to myself at that one. Then I remembered that I had a book about marketing oneself that I had gotten at one of those company retreats. I ran upstairs to flip through my bookshelf. I knew I had kept that book.

As I pulled a stack off the bookshelf, the chakra book that Colbie had given me fell out of the pile. *Chakras & You – How to Understand the Energy Within.* I opened the book and noticed that Colbie had written something.

Evie,

*Understanding your chakras will serve you
well. Energy gets blocked sometimes. This will
help you understand your energy and how to keep
it flowing.*
    In peace,
    Colbie

I started to flip through the pages. Seven chakras: Root (Red), Cervix (Orange), Solar Plexus (Yellow), Heart (Green), Throat (Blue), Third Eye (Indigo), Crown (Purple). I skimmed through and landed on the crown chakra. I thought of Colbie and how she embodied the characteristics of the crown—knowledge, consciousness, spirituality.

For the next two hours, I devoured the book. It kind of made sense, but how did I use it? How did I know if I was blocked? Still so much to learn.

Standing up, I stretched then walked through the house. Now that I had gotten rid of so much stuff, the house seemed even larger than before.

"What am I doing?" I asked myself out loud. "Why am I here?" I needed a fresh start. I needed a new environment.

Right at that moment, I decided to sell my house. I didn't need all of this. I could get a nice townhouse somewhere and happily paint for the rest of my life. Plus, I should also make a substantial return on the house since everyone and their brother was moving from Texas to Colorado. The market was blowing up, so I might as well take advantage. Luckily, my house was in great shape, other than the paint-splattered walls in my studio. That should be an easy fix.

I called the realtor who had sold me the house six years ago. He was a great guy, who had kept in touch over the years. So, his tenacity paid off.

"Hi, Matt. This is Evie," I greeted.

"Hi, Evie. How are you doing?"

"I am wonderful, and I want to sell my house," I blurted.

"Whoa, okay. That's great. So, how can I help you?"

"Would you be willing to be my realtor?"

"Of course I would. Thank you for thinking of me. Your timing is great. As you may know, it's a hot market in Colorado right now. Plus, you live in a great school district. How soon would you like me to come by so I can check out the house, take photos, etcetera?"

"Anytime. I would like to sell as is. I don't want to have to do any work. Plus, the house is in great shape to begin with," I told him.

"Great. How about tomorrow at ten?"

"That sounds perfect. See you tomorrow."

"Yes, looking forward to it," he said before hanging up.

Wow, I couldn't believe that I had just decided to sell my house. Now what did I do? Where would I go? I was definitely not one of those tiny house, convert an old school bus into my home kind of person. I still need a little space. I guessed I could move farther out of town and find a small property somewhere.

Then I heard, "*Go to where you learned to paint,*" as a warm energy came over me.

Of course! I could go back to my grandparents' house. It would be full circle. Plus, I already owned it.

Having a plan really kicked me into action. I walked around my house, assessing what I wanted to take and what should stay. I didn't want to hire a moving truck, so I needed to scale down to what I could fit into a U-Haul.

I sent texts to Colbie, Hendrix, and Reva, telling them the news, and asked Colbie and Hendrix if they wanted to stop by and take any items that I would not be bringing with me. To some, this might seem really fast, but when it felt so good and right, things just fell into place.

I decided I didn't really need any furniture, as the house on the island was fully furnished. After my grandfather had passed away, I had found out that he hadn't had a will, so everything had gone to the state. I hadn't wanted to lose the house, as it was the only thing left of my family, so I had bought it. However, I hadn't had the time to clean it out, so I was sure there was plenty of furniture that I could use.

I took inventory of what I would not be taking. If Colbie or Hendrix didn't want it, I would offer it to be sold with the house.

My phone rang. I picked it up and all I heard was, *"What?"*

"Hi, Hendrix."

"Wow, when you jump, you really jump," he exclaimed.

"Go big or go home, so I have decided to go home. I don't need all this stuff, and I don't need this huge house, so I'm selling."

"Where are you going?" he asked.

"I am moving back East. I don't know if I told you, but I own my grandparents' house on Martha's Vineyard. I am going to be an island girl again."

"How wonderful, but I am going to miss you, Evie."

"Don't worry; headhunters, or passion hunters, need to vacation, too, don't they? You are more than welcome to come and visit. Honestly, I hope you do," I said. *Where did that come from?* "I have a funny feeling that this sale will not take long, so I wanted to invite you over to see if there was any furniture that you would like to have. I am only bringing the bare minimum."

"Sure, how about later this week? Thursday work?" he asked.

"Perfect. See you then."

Not long after I spoke with Hendrix, Colbie called.

"What is happening? What are you doing?" she probed.

I proceed to give her the rundown on what had happened and where I was going. She was sad to see me leave, but incredibly happy that I was creating the life that I wanted to live. We planned for her to stop by late Thursday afternoon.

Last but not least, Reva called.

"Damn, girl, you sound wonderful, and I know this move is going to be great for you. Congratulations!"

"Thank you. I think so, as well. Plus, we are going to be closer now. You can be one of the many New Yorkers who vacation on the island."

She laughed. "Don't think I won't take you up on that offer. After this pandemic is done, I need to get out of this city."

I gave her an account of my next steps and told her that I would let her know when I hit the road.

Before we hung up, she said, "Evie, I am so proud of you."

So, that was it. Plans made and friends told. I would tell Tatum on Wednesday and, hopefully, have this house sold within a couple of weeks.

CHAPTER 8 — BACK EAST

I worked through the rest of the night, packing, cleaning, and organizing. I planned to drop by the moving store tomorrow to pick up boxes to pack what little belongings I would be taking with me.

Matt arrived right on time and took a look around the house.

"Wow, Evie, this place is in great shape. Except for the paint-splattered room, everything looks perfect. We should be able to get a great price for this house. Because the market has been so crazy lately, I don't think we should have any problem with an as-is sale."

"Good, because I don't want to do anything but move my stuff out. I have some friends coming over on Thursday to take a look at my furniture. What they don't take, I would like to include in the sales price," I explained.

"Well, I checked the comps in the neighborhood, and I believe that we could easily ask seven hundred thousand. Let me take some pictures, and we can get this listed tonight."

"Perfect. I will leave you to it. Just yell if you need any help."

Within an hour, Matt found me upstairs in my bedroom.

"Evie," he yelled out, "I'm done.

"Wonderful."

"I think I got some great pictures, and the fact that you still have your furniture is great, so we didn't even have to stage the house. So, we good with seven hundred thousand?" he asked.

"Yes, I think that is a great price."

"All right then, I will text you when the listing goes live. I have a funny feeling this is going to go quickly. So, do you know where you're going?"

I grinned. "Yup, I am heading back East. The day we close is the day I start my drive."

After Matt left, I jumped into my car and headed over to the moving company to buy some boxes, tape, and packing materials. I also got pricing information for a trailer.

After I bought the packing supplies, I decided to take a drive around town for one last real look at Denver.

Things had really changed since I had moved here six year ago. There were parts that I would definitely miss, like seeing the snow-covered mountain range. My skin would finally love me again, being at sea level. My hair, on the other hand, would probably revolt.

I found the drive to be so pleasant and relaxing. I was seeing things that I had never seen before. It wasn't like they were new or just built; I had just never really looked when I had driven around before, always in a rush to get to where I was going. Too bad I didn't stop and smell the roses more often.

As I headed home, I got this urge to get off two exits earlier than I would have. I was driving down the street when, all of a sudden, I saw Triniti walking by.

I slowed down and yelled out the window, "Triniti, hey. It's Evie."

She looked over in shock, but then she gave me a huge smile. "Evie, what are you doing around here?"

"I got an urge to turn down this street, and guess what? I run into you. So, how are you doing?"

I heard a honk behind me and realized that I had just stopped in the middle of the street.

I let the car pass then asked Triniti to give me a second so I could park. Luckily, there was a spot just a few feet away.

I walked back to Triniti, asking, "So, how are you doing?"

"I'm doing great. Life gets better every day." She smiled widely. "And, how are you doing?"

"Amazing. I am getting ready to move back East. Putting my house on the market and will head out as soon as it sells."

"Where to back East?" she asked.

"Oh, I have a house on Martha's Vineyard, so I will be moving to the island to paint."

Triniti's mouth dropped open, and then she started laughing. A big booming laugh, which was a huge surprise coming from such a petite body.

I giggled. "What's so funny?"

When she finally caught her breath, she looked at me with a glint in her eyes. "That's why you were told to turn down my street. I grew up on the Vineyard."

"What?" I yelled. "No way."

"Yup. Born and raised. After college, I moved out here with my then boyfriend. Things did not work out, fortunately. I decided to stay, but I go home at least once every year. Generally, in the summer. I need to see the ocean, eat lobster, and feel the humidity," she confided.

"Well, if you are going home this summer, please look me up," I told her. We then exchanged phone numbers and promised that we would get together this summer.

"Have a great drive, and I will see you this summer," Triniti called out as I drove away.

In the car, I just started laughing and asked out loud, "Higher self, do you ever do anything in a straight line?"

I smiled, knowing that it was the experience that I was here to have, so I answered my own question.

When I got home, I checked my phone. Matt had just pinged me to let me know that the listing was live. Well, there was no turning back now.

I remembered, when I had moved from Chicago to Denver, I had been so nervous. No friends or family, but I had been moving for a job, so there was some safety. The whole process had seemed so much greater than what I was about to do now. It was ironic since I was selling my house, driving across country solo, and moving to an island where I had only lived briefly, to follow my dream to be a full-time artist. My former self would be freaking out right now. So, why was I so calm?

Because it just felt right.

When I got home, I saw Sue walking to her car. She stopped and waited until I parked then called out, "Need help with those boxes?"

"Yes, that would be great," I replied. This was the first time in six years that Sue had wanted to engage with me. It was funny, but I welcomed it.

She grabbed the packing materials, and I grabbed the boxes.

When we got into the house, I said, "You can put that stuff on the kitchen table."

"I had a funny feeling when you had your garage sale that you would be moving," she remarked. "Do you mind if I take a look around? I am always so curious of how the different models look."

"No worries. Have at it," I replied.

I could hear Sue walking around, and then she reappeared in the kitchen.

"So, I assume the bedroom upstairs was your painting studio." She laughed. Then she looked around the kitchen and said, "Oh, Evie, did you paint that?" She was looking at the small painting that I had done of the vase that Triniti had given me. "That is so beautiful."

"Thank you."

"Well, you are definitely talented." She then turned to me with a profoundly serious look on her face. "How did you get so brave?"

"What do you mean?" I questioned.

"You have no fear. You lose your job, but instead of looking for a new one, you decide to go in a completely different direction as an artist. I'm no expert, but I don't know many wealthy artists. Actually, I don't know any artists, other than you, but you only hear of the really famous dead ones. How are you going to survive?"

"I am working with a person who will help me sell my work, and I am taking a leap of faith. Instead of betting on a company to take care of me, I am betting on myself. I have an incredibly good friend who shared a very poignant quote with me about a bird trusting its wings and not the branch it was perched on. When I was ready to hear it, it all made sense to me."

"I wish I could be so strong," she said. "I would love to be a florist, but …" She trailed off.

"But what?" I asked. "Sue, no offense, but none of us are getting any younger. Do you want to be an accountant all your life? Crunching someone else's numbers? Do you think the people that own your favorite florist are any different than you?"

"No, not really," she replied.

"Then, why do you think they can be successful and you can't?" I asked. "They had a dream, and they took the leap of faith and bet on themselves. You can do the same."

"But I am too scared," she admitted.

"Believe you me; I understand that fear. I am still scared about this move and my new life. But, if you can remove the fear of the unknown and turn it into an adventure, it makes it easier. I am confident that I will land on my feet. In the end, will I be an artist? Maybe. What I do know is that I will only do things that make me happy from now on."

Sue looked at me, her eyes searching my face, genuinely wanting to believe.

To reassure her, I said, "If you are not ready to take the leap, do small things that will lead you down that path. Maybe see if you can work part-time at a florist or take a flower arranging class. There are so many things you can do to feed your passion.

Then, one day, you will know it is time. Also, ask your higher self for guidance. You will be amazed that, when you ask, you will receive an answer."

"Evie, thank you for the guidance. I know we haven't been close, but I was wondering if we can keep in touch?"

"Of course," I answered, trying to disguise my surprise.

We exchanged contact information, and then she gave me a hug, wishing me the best of luck, and walked out.

I didn't know if the sadness that I felt in that moment was because the move was becoming real or that I understood the confusion that she felt right now. Either way, we both were better for the decisions that we made to create the lives that we desired.

After packing a few boxes, I looked at the clock and saw it was six thirty. No wonder I was so hungry. I looked in the refrigerator, seeing I had nothing to eat, I decided to grab my favorite poke. First, I stopped in the bathroom.

It seemed like I hadn't looked in the mirror all day, and it showed. My hair was indescribable. I was always so particular about my hair, too—getting it trimmed every six weeks. But, since the pandemic, I hadn't been able to get a regular cut. I had been making do, but boy, I was a mess.

I tried to fix my hair but quickly gave up and threw on a ball cap. No need to change my clothes, as I was taking my food to-go.

I pulled into the parking lot of the poke shop and saw what I thought to be Hendrix's car. Sure enough, just as I was about to walk in, Hendrix walked out. My head was down, so I didn't even realize it until I heard his voice.

"Evie?"

I looked up. "Hendrix, what are you doing here?"

"Well, I remember you ordering from here a while back and thought I would give it a try."

"Nice. I love this place." I smiled then gestured at his to-go bag. "Well, I don't want to keep you from it. Are we still good for Thursday?"

"Actually, I won't be able to come by on Thursday. I have a new corporate client who I need to meet. But I would love to see what you have. I could use an update to my current bachelor pad."

"Well, if you don't mind waiting, you could come over now, and we could eat dinner at my place," I offered.

"That would be wonderful," He beamed. "I would really like that. Do you see my car over there? Wave to me when you are done, and I will follow you over."

"Great," I replied.

He held the door open for me as I went in.

I blushed a bit and said, "Thank you."

As I walked to the counter, I was sure I looked like a crazy person, talking to myself. Actually, I was talking out loud, thinking that what I was saying was only in my head.

"I can't believe I just did that. I look like shit, and Hendrix is coming over."

"Hi. Can I help you?" the server asked. "And, by the way, you don't look like shit."

I blushed even more. "Thank you. May I have the Hawaiian with salmon, extra roe, and a seaweed salad, please?"

Walking out of the shop a few minutes later, I saw Hendrix and waved.

He watched me get in my car then followed me to the house.

I tried to fix my hair and straighten my clothes while I drove, but it was no use. I was what I was.

I pulled into the garage, and Hendrix left his car in the driveway.

He followed me into the kitchen, saying, "Hey, beautiful house."

"Thank you. It's a bit upside down right now."

As we sat at the kitchen table to enjoy our bowls, Hendrix asked, "How is the packing going? Has there been any interest on the house yet?"

That was when I realized that this was the first real opportunity, outside of a quick coffee, that Hendrix and I'd had in person with each other that wasn't work related.

We had met when I had first arrived in Colorado. He had served as our subject matter expert on a software sales campaign that we had been creating for his company. I had always been impressed with him, as he was so kind and understanding. His demeanor didn't always match his exterior, but when you looked into his eyes, you knew that he was a loving person.

"Packing is good. House literally just went on the market an hour ago," I answered.

We made more small talk, which was nice, and then, after we finished our dinners and were throwing our take-out containers in the trash, I asked, "Do you want to see the furniture?"

"Sure," he said, wiping his hands off on a tea towel.

As we walked through the house, Hendrix said, "Evie, this place is so big. Has it always been just you here?"

"Yup. I thought about getting a dog at some point, but I was always working, so it wouldn't have been fair to keep it crated for hours on end." I answered.

"So," I changed the subject, "is there anything in particular that you are needing? I have a great living room set, if you are interested?"

As we walked into the living room so that I could show him the furniture, he saw my paintings leaning against the wall.

"Wow, Evie, is this your work?"

"Yes." I felt my cheeks get a little warm.

"These are absolutely magnificent. I can feel so much emotion." He stopped and just stared at me with this beautiful, warm smile. "I am so happy that you have found your passion and are pursuing it. It takes a lot of courage to take the leap, but it is so worth it."

"Well, I have to thank you for your guidance. I would never have been able to get here if it wasn't for you, and a few other people. This is such a new world, but I am enjoying the ride. I must ask you, though: how long have you been on your journey?"

"My journey started a long time ago. My upbringing was not what bedtime stories were written about. After one very abusive evening, I thought about committing suicide. As I lay there, all bloody and bruised, I heard a voice that said, '*Know me, and I will protect you.*' When I first heard it, I didn't know if I was alive or dead. At the age of eleven, you can't really tell people that you are hearing voices. You can barely talk about it now. But, from that day on, as I learned more, I was never in that kind of a situation again. I studied, meditated, and talked to happy people. Through all this, I was able to release the pain that I had experienced and learned how to create my life," he explained.

"Oh no. I am so sorry."

"No need to say that, Evie. We all come to this earth to experience life to its fullest. That doesn't always mean lollipops and unicorns. Experience is just that—good, bad, happy, or sad. I have learned to enjoy the experience, and if it is not to my liking, then asking why or what am I supposed to be learning from it.

"As we have talked about before, we are all energy. Sometimes, unknowingly, our energy is focused on something that we don't want or that we fear. When the energy is strong, that thing that we don't want will actually come to fruition, if we focus on it long enough. So, this life is a journey. You have to be mindful of what you think about and focus on. There will be twists and turns, setbacks and advances, but it is all life that you are here to experience. There is a quote from Winifred Gallagher that I try to live by:

> *"Living the focused life is not about trying to feel happy all the time; rather it is about treating your mind as you would a private garden and*

*being as careful as possible about what you
introduce and allow to grow there."*

"I am so relieved to hear you say that," I told him. "Even
though this move feels right, I will admit I do have a bit of fear
of the unknown. I tell myself, *enjoy the ride and make the
unknown an adventure* but, at times, I don't feel strong enough
to believe my own hype," I admitted.

"The first step is that you recognize you have the fear. From
there, you can change your energy. But you have to believe or,
better yet, know that all will turn out how it is supposed to.
Remember that you don't have to do this by yourself. You have
the ability to ask for guidance. The more you ask, the more you
receive. Just remember to follow the guidance."

I smiled. "Thank you. So"—I laughed— "are you interested
in the living room furniture?"

"Actually, I am. This will really make me look like I'm
grownup." He laughed. "So, what are you asking for it?"

"Nothing. If you want it, it's yours."

He gave me a gentle smile. "Evie, that is very generous."

"Just trying to lighten my load. I am moving into a house
that is well-furnished, so I am trying to downsize, not add more.
All you have to do is move it, and it is yours."

"I can have a truck over here tomorrow, if that works for
you?" he replied.

"That would be great. I will be out all morning, but after
that, I will be around."

"Then it's a date. I will see you tomorrow afternoon. I'll call
when we are heading over."

I walked Hendrix to the door and thanked him for the
company. He gave me that beautiful smile and asked if he could
have a hug. I happily obliged. It was one of those big, warm hugs
that, admittedly, lasted a little longer than I had expected, but I
wasn't going to stop if he wasn't. When we finally separated, I
almost couldn't look him in the eyes. We said our goodbyes, and
then I watched him drive off.

When I closed the door, I squealed and danced around a bit. Such amazing energy that man had. I just loved it.

For the rest of the evening, I was in the clouds, just floating around.

Right before I went to bed, I checked my phone. There was an email from Matt, saying he already had a number of interested buyers and asking if he could start showing the house tomorrow morning. I emailed him back, saying I could be out of the house by eight thirty but needed to be back around one. Matt was quick to respond, saying he would be at the house by eight thirty to grab the keys.

I put my phone down, turned off the light, and rolled over. Next thing I knew, I was watching a couple walk along a beach on the island, holding hands. It was like I was watching a movie, but I could only see their backs. Even though I couldn't see who the man was, I knew the woman was me.

***

As soon as I woke up, I started moving boxes out of the middle of the floor and into the closets, the garage, and anywhere else they would fit. Then I straightened up, washed the dishes, and moved my paintings into the studio. They might as well know that there was an artist living here.

Once everything was put away and cleaned up, I jumped into the shower. I had to look presentable, as I would be meeting Tatum at eleven, and I wouldn't have the opportunity to come back to the house beforehand.

I looked in my closet. All I seemed to have were suits, blouses, or gym wear. Nothing I would call entrepreneur casual. I ended up putting on jean trousers—my go-to for office Friday dress down day—and a T-shirt with a blazer. Then I looked in the mirror. *This will work*, I thought to myself.

As I brushed my teeth, I realized that it is just about eight thirty, so I quickly rinsed, grabbed my jacket, mask, phone, and bag, and headed toward the door. But, as I reached for the door handle, the bell rang, scaring the bejesus out of me.

Matt, right on time, as always.

I opened the door. "Good morning, Matt."

"Good morning. Ready for a big day?" He beamed.

"I guess I should ask you the same thing. Ready to sell my house?"

"I definitely am. There has been a *lot* of interest. I have four showings just this morning. This may all be said and done by the end of the week." He smiled.

"Wow, that is good news. Oh, wanted you to know that the living room furniture is spoken for, if anyone asks," I warned.

"Got it."

I handed my spare keys to Matt then headed out the door.

Just as I was pulling away, a car parked outside the house, the first showing.

So, it was only eight forty-five, and I didn't have my meeting until eleven. What to do? It wasn't like everything was open yet, not only because of the hour, but we were still in a pandemic.

I drove into downtown to see if there was a good breakfast place open. I should have thought this out better. Since the pandemic, there had been a lot of restaurant closings. If they were open, they had limited hours. I finally found an open bagel shop, grabbed an everything with cream cheese and a nice cup of coffee, and took it to the park to eat.

Though the morning was still brisk, it was nice to sit outside on a park bench. Life was returning to downtown. People were jogging, walking their dogs, and heading to work. If this was a year and a half ago, I wouldn't want to even be downtown. The traffic would have been a nightmare, and you couldn't ever find parking. Now it was much quieter and, in a sense, nicer.

After I ate my bagel, I closed my eyes and took the opportunity to do my morning meditation. When I quieted my mind, I heard, *"You will share your life with someone."*

Then I remembered my dream and asked, "Who?"

I was told it was not time yet, that I would soon know.

Hmm ... a relationship. I hadn't had one of those for a long while. I sometimes allowed myself to think about *what if* ... but then I would shut it down because it never seemed like I had time to meet someone. Reva was always willing to set me up, but I never took her up on the offer.

The thought of having someone in my life put me in such a wonderful space that I didn't realize that it was almost eleven already.

I grabbed my coffee and bag then headed back to the car. Since there wasn't traffic, I had more than enough time to get to the coffee shop to meet Tatum, so I took the scenic route back to my neighborhood.

The morning had warmed up nicely, and I once again found a great table outside to wait for Tatum. She arrived just a few minutes after me and greeted me with a wonderful hug.

"So, you ready to build your business?" she asked.

"Yes, I am. But first, I have to let you know that I am in the process of selling my house and moving back East," I replied.

"Whoa, okay. That is a surprise. Business-wise, it's no big deal, but I want to hear how this all came about."

I gave her a rundown on how this all happened.

"Well, what a wonderful opportunity for you. As someone who is interested in your success, I am glad to see that you are creating an atmosphere that will encourage creativity. The more pieces you paint, the more opportunity I have to sell," she commented with a grin.

"Speaking of selling, I was able to speak with the two individuals who I thought would be interested in your paintings." Tatum stood up. "I am happy to announce that both paintings are officially sold." She then started clapping and bringing a lot of attention to us from passersby.

I jumped up, too. "Really? Both of them?"

"Yes, and for the full asking price!"

We hugged and started jumping around. Anyone who walked by the coffee shop would have thought we had won the lottery by the amount of noise we were making.

I fell back into my seat and said, "Oh my gosh, I can't believe that they really sold. I mean, I had high hopes, but I have been here before, and it didn't turn out well."

"Evie, things are different now; you have to know that. It is up to you to set your course. If you are an artist, be an artist. Know that you create amazing art and know that it will sell. Working from this knowing mindset creates amazing outcomes. So, now that you have two paintings that have sold, let's get you set up with a website and get you on social media," she concluded.

We talked for almost two hours, creating my marketing strategy. Then Tatum said she would swing by on Friday to pick up the paintings and to deliver the checks.

She was definitely a person who I was glad to have in my life. I knew she was running a business, but I genuinely believed that she would do anything to help me be successful. What a difference from my former work life.

I put my hand over my heart and told her, "Thank you." Then we hugged, and I hurried to my car, needing to get back to the house to meet Hendrix.

Just as I was pulling into my driveway, my phone rang.

"Hey, Evie, we are on our way," Hendrix announced.

"Great. I literally just got home myself. See you in a few."

When I opened the door and walked in, I felt something. It was almost like a heaviness in the house. It was such an unusual sensation. Not good or bad; just different. I realized that I could feel the energy of the people who had been in my house. I hadn't had visitors since this whole pandemic had started, except for when Hendrix and I'd had dinner. That energy was amazing. This energy was mixed, and I felt out of sorts by it.

I put my bags down on the kitchen table then went to the studio to look at my paintings. I noticed there was a piece of paper leaning up against one of them that read: "*Do these paintings come with the house?*" I smiled and said out loud, "Sorry, they are officially sold."

To finally be able to say that gave me such a jolt of energy. It made me forget about having complete strangers walking through my house, and it made me realize that I really was doing the right thing with my life.

I changed clothes then went down to the living room, checking drawers and shelves to make sure that I didn't leave anything. Then I lifted the cushions of the couch and chairs to see if anything important had fallen between and to also make sure that there were no missing French fries. I grabbed the vacuum and cleaned up any crumbs that I had left behind. Boy, when this left, I was going to have a lot of room to roam around in. I might move my yoga mat down here.

As I stood there, daydreaming, I heard a truck pull into the driveway. I looked out the front window and saw Hendrix getting out of the truck. There was also a young lady with him.

I felt myself gasp for air. *Who was that?*

I opened the door and went out to say hello. Before I reached him, however, I was greeted by the young lady. Her smile was enormous, with bright white, beautiful teeth and a glint in her eyes.

"Hi, Evie. I'm Nichole, Hendrix's sister. It is so nice to meet you. I have heard so much about you," she gushed.

"Oh, hi, Nichole, Hendrix's sister. So nice to meet you, too," I responded, hoping I hadn't shown my relief when I'd said it.

"It is so nice of you to give this furniture to Hendrix. I have been telling him for years that he really should turn that bachelor pad into a home now that he is getting older." She said the last bit loud enough for Hendrix to hear. Then she laughed and winked at me.

Hendrix came around the truck and greeted me with one of his wonderful, big, warm hugs. I tried to not enjoy it too much, as his sister was watching.

"Evie, thank you again for your generosity. I have to agree with my sister that it is time that I turn my bachelor pad into a home, but it is not because I am getting older." He looked at her as he said it. "I am expecting two other friends to be here any minute to help lift everything," he added.

"No problem. I am done with all my meetings for the day. All I'm doing now is packing, so no rush."

As we waited for Hendrix's friends, Nichole started to ask me questions.

"So, Evie, you are moving back East to be an artist?"

"She is already an artist," Hendrix butt in.

"Thank you," I told him then said to his sister, "Yes, I am moving to Martha's Vineyard to live in my grandparents' house and to paint."

"That is so cool," she said. "I hear this is a big move."

"Well, it kind of is. I am starting a new adventure and following my heart."

"I love hearing about people following their hearts. I know, when Hendrix made his big move to be a headhunter, he actually turned into a nice person again. Not to say that you are not a nice person," she quickly added. "What I am trying to say is that Hendrix realized what made him happy, and now he is really successful."

"Nichole, if it wasn't for your brother, and a few other people, I probably wouldn't be taking this leap of faith. My desire is to be as happy and successful as he is."

"By the way that Hendrix talks about your paintings, it seems impossible that you won't be successful."

I found myself blushing and turned away quickly. Luckily for me, Hendrix's friends pulled up just then and honked the horn.

"Hey, Hendrix," one of them yelled out the window.

"Travis, thanks for helping, man," Hendrix replied.

Two well-built gentlemen came walking up the driveway.

Travis yelled out, "Hey, Nik. Long time, no see."

"Hey, Travis," Nichole responded weakly.

Hendrix shook both men's hands and said, "Travis, Leon, I would like you to meet my friend, Evie."

I said hello to both men, and they both fist-pumped me and said hello back. Then I led the group into the house and to the living room, pointing out all the furniture that Hendrix would be taking.

"Wow, this is really nice stuff, and she is just giving it away?" I heard Leon say under his breath.

In no time, the four of them had all the furniture out of the house and in the driveway. Hendrix was figuring out how to get it all into his truck as the guys loaded the furniture.

Nichole came over to me. "Evie, I was making fun of my brother before, but please know how much he appreciates what you are doing for him and know that he is going to really miss you."

"It's no big deal. I am downsizing, and I was more than happy to give this to him. He is a wonderful man, and he has helped me grow in so many ways," I explained.

Hendrix finished tying down the furniture then walked over to Nichole and me. "Hey, Nik, I'll meet you in the truck."

He then yelled over to Travis and Leon, "Meet you guys at my house."

As his friends drove away, I heard them yell out, "Nice to meet you, Evie."

Hendrix looked back at me. "So, any news on the house yet?"

"Matt, my real estate agent, says that he showed the house to four people already. There is a lot of interest, so it will move fast," I answered.

"Well, when you know what day you are leaving, please let me know. I would love to be able to say a proper goodbye."

In my head, I thought, *What is a proper goodbye?* but I didn't say it out loud.

My heart started pounding. It thumped so loud that I swear Hendrix could hear it. I tried to play it off by casually saying, "I definitely will. And enjoy the furniture."

He gave me another one of those amazing hugs then said, "Talk to you soon."

OMG, I felt like a little girl. What was happening to me?

I responded in a squeaky voice, "Yes, talk to you soon."

When I walked back into the house, it felt empty and even echoed. *Hmm ... this is really happening*, I said to myself.

I strolled into the kitchen to make something to eat, and as I sat down, I started going through my emails. That was when a text from Matt popped up.

"Please call me. Great news!"

I stopped mid-bite and called Matt.

"Hey, Evie. Thanks for calling so quickly. The showings went amazing today, and we have two offers at full price."

"Two offers? That's great."

"Unless you want to decide out of the two, which you probably don't, I would like to go back to both of them and say that I need their best offers. Whoever comes in higher gets the house. Sound like a plan?" he asked.

"Yeah, that sounds like a great plan."

"Okay, I will call you tomorrow. Have a great night and start packing!" he exclaimed.

With all the room that I now had in my living room, I ran, jumped up, and clicked my heels. It was all working out.

I put my hand over my heart center and said, "Thank you!"

Walking around the house, I realized that I really did have most of my stuff packed. Right now, I counted thirty plus boxes. I hoped Colbie would be interested in my kitchen table and chairs, and maybe my bedroom furniture. If not, I could see if Tatum needed anything and check in with Triniti, as she was still getting back on her feet.

I jumped in the shower, relaxing in the warm water. Today had been a good day. I ran through all that had happened and gave thanks to my higher self for guiding me. Then I started to wonder about Hendrix.

Was he the man who I had seen in my dream? Was he the one who I would have a relationship with? That would be nice. Nichole's comments had definitely been a surprise, but they were such nice, open people that I could be reading way more into it than there really was. Time would tell.

I turned off the shower and got ready for bed.

CHAPTER 9 — DECLARE IT

It was already Wednesday. Wow, this week was flying by. Colbie should be here this morning to look at my furniture, and I still needed to book a moving truck and continue packing.

I rolled out of bed and right to the floor, gratefully entering my morning meditation.

As I started to clear my mind, I heard, *"Walk in nature."*

My initial response was that I had too much to do, but then I stopped myself and trusted that I had the time to take a walk in nature today.

Since I was already on the floor, I did my morning stretches to get the blood flowing and the body loosened up. As I rose into my mountain pose, I caught a glimpse of myself in the mirror. It was amazing how different I looked. My skin glowed, and the ever-present bags under my eyes had disappeared. I looked younger, rested and, dare I say, happy?

I declared that today was a good day, that I would enjoy it.

As I headed into the kitchen, I grabbed my phone and saw that Matt had texted me, saying he would have final offers by this afternoon.

After breakfast, I went back to packing. Colbie should be here in about a half an hour. I looked forward to seeing her. I hadn't really made a lot of good friends in Colorado. Mostly work associates. Plus, I had traveled so much that I was able to see Reva often, and when I wasn't on the road, all I had wanted to do was be at home and sleep. Had I truly taken advantage of what Colorado had to offer? No, but even if I had done more things, I didn't know if I would have appreciated them. I had gone through much of my life seeing things but not really seeing anything. I had always been traveling for work, in hotels, in meeting rooms, but I had never given myself the opportunity to be where I was, to experience and to feel. I was always running, looking at what was next.

Living in the present had given me the opportunity to see, feel, and experience more than I ever had. The first half of my adult life was a bit of a blur, but the second half would be enlightening.

I heard the doorbell ring and saw it was Colbie. Opening the door, I gave her a huge hug, almost knocking her over.

"Wow, that's a hell of a greeting," she commented. "How are you doing?"

"I am wonderful, and I am so glad that you are here. Come in, come in." I gestured for her to come inside.

Colbie walked through the door while saying, "Well, I guess this is real. All of your stuff is gone."

"Not *all* of my stuff. I was hoping that you would be interested in my kitchen table, chairs, or my bedroom set, or anything else that you see."

"I don't need anything for the kitchen, but I would love to see your bedroom set. Prior to Dan's death, we updated every other room in the house but always left our bedroom for last. The kids' needs took precedent. I would love to create a little oasis for myself."

"Great. Follow me." I took Colbie's hand and, like an excited little kid, almost dragged her up the stairs to the bedroom.

As we walked into my bedroom, I said, "Ta da! Will this work for you?"

Colbie just stopped and stared, finally saying "Geez, Evie, this set is beautiful. Please remind me why you are not taking this with you."

"I am moving to my grandparents' house that is already full. I need to weed through their stuff, and I just didn't want to add more to what I already know is a lot. Plus, I would like a fresh start."

"Well, that is good for me. Sold!" she exclaimed. "How much?"

"Great. I am so glad that you like it and that you can use it. My gift to you. As I am learning, you need to take care of yourself."

Colbie smiled. "Thank you. Now the issue is *how* to get this stuff out of here and to my house. How soon do you need me to move it?" she asked.

"I would say no later than this weekend. I am supposed to hear from my agent this afternoon. I already have two offers on the house. So, I would assume that we will close by next Monday."

"Boy, when you set your mind to something, it happens," she commented.

I grinned at her. "Well, isn't that what everyone has been telling me? I declare it, and my higher self is the GPS guiding me step by step. This whole process has felt right and, to be completely honest, I am enjoying it, as well. To know that you and others are so grateful for these items gives me immense joy. These things were just stuff to me, but for you and others, it is a new start. I love being able to help."

"Thank you, Evie, and I do appreciate the help. Do you still have a lot to do here?" she wondered.

"Why?"

"I was going to take a hike. Needed to get some fresh air. Do you want to join me?"

A big smile appeared on my face.

"Why are you smiling?" Colbie questioned.

"I was told to take a walk in nature today, so yes, I would love to join you."

We jumped into her SUV and headed up to Red Rocks.

As we drove, I complained, "I can't believe I never saw a concert here."

"It's been years since I have seen a concert here, but I can't imagine seeing a concert inside. Music with the mountains as a backdrop is spectacular."

When we arrived, we wound up the road and parked in one of the lower parking lots. We decide to walk the seats first to get the blood pumping then hike the small trail around the venue.

"It feels so good to be out here," I commented. "I definitely needed this break."

"Good. I thought you may need a little downtime with all that you are doing, and I wanted for us to make another memory of our friendship." She beamed at me.

"Thank you. This really is special."

We did the short hike and found a beautiful spot to just rest and take in the scenery.

"So, Colbie, how are you and the boys doing since Dan's death?" I inquired.

"It is lonely at times," she started. "But, whenever I really need to feel him, I ask that he give me a sign. He always does. The boys understand that it was just Dan's flesh and blood that left them, that his soul is with them forever, but they can't help, and neither can I, missing the flesh and blood part of him. There are times when I just want to smell him or hear his goofy laugh."

"I have experience death in my life, but I did not handle it as well as you are handling Dan's death. That is a lesson that I need to learn. Going back to my grandparents' place—I guess I should say my place—will bring up a lot of memories. Not all good. There are so many things that I did not understand, and they did not explain to me about my mother's death."

"Just remember, they are with you, even your mother. All you have to do is ask."

"I am almost afraid to. I don't know if I really want to know."

Colbie placed her hand on my arm and, with what seemed like an angelic voice, said, "When the time comes that you do, just remember it was her journey and you have your own."

I smiled at her. "You always make me feel so connected. I so love that about you. I hope that we stay in touch and that you and the boys can find some time to come out and visit."

"Oh, they we would love that," she replied.

A few hours later, after a wonderful drive and hike, we returned to my house and said our goodbyes. Colbie said she would call tomorrow to arrange a time to pick up the bedroom furniture. Secretly, I was glad she hadn't taken it today, as I still needed something to sleep on.

I walked into an empty house. Well, I still had a kitchen table and chairs, and a few other pieces of furniture that I needed to find homes for.

I grabbed my phone and gave Triniti a call.

"Evie, are you already on the Vineyard?" she asked.

"No, not yet, but soon. I was wondering if you are still in need of furniture. I have a kitchen table set and some other odds and ends that I need to find a home for. Interested?" I probed.

Almost before I could finish my sentence, she exclaimed, "Yes! The bedroom set you gave me is the nicest piece of furniture I have ever owned. It really stands out next to all the other dumpster dive pieces that I have. Can I stop by tomorrow to pick them up?" she inquired.

"Sure. What time?"

"If you don't mind, I can do it early, like eight thirty. My friend doesn't have to be to work until ten, so that should give us plenty of time," she stated.

"Okay, see you at eight thirty tomorrow."

"Evie, you have been a life saver. Seriously, thank you."

"My pleasure."

I hung up with Triniti, and then Matt called a few minutes later.

"Evie, so I have some great news. The two couples came back and gave their final offers. One came in at seven hundred and twenty-five thousand dollars and the other—drum roll please."—he paused for dramatic effect—"at seven hundred and fifty thousand. I assume you are okay with the seven hundred-and-fifty-thousand-dollar offer."

I was so dumbfounded that I didn't answer him for at least thirty seconds.

"Evie? Evie, you there?" he questioned.

"Yes, yes, I am. Holy shit, I can't believe they offered seven hundred and fifty thousand," I said.

"Oh, and they want all the appliances, but no furniture," he added.

"Phew, good, because I have given all the furniture away." I laughed.

"Great. I will schedule the closing for Monday, if that works for you?" he proposed.

"Monday works perfectly. Can we make the closing mid-morning so I can hit the road by the afternoon?"

"Will do my best," he responded.

We hung up, and then I just sat there, amazed at what had just happened. This would give me a nice nest egg to pull from as I got the island house in order and my painting business up and running.

***

For the rest of the evening, I packed and labeled boxes. I had them all stacked up in the living room. I might be able to pull off a small U-Haul trailer, if I kept on giving things away.

As I looked around the house, I saw it was just a shell. It echoed and didn't feel warm at all.

I made myself my usual peanut butter and honey sandwich then sat at my kitchen table one last time. My television was gone, so I looked at social media, watched a little Dodo, and then called it a night.

I crawled into bed then realized that I was supposed to tell Hendrix when I was leaving so he could give me a "proper goodbye." Instead of calling him, though, I sent him a text, saying that I would be heading out on Monday afternoon.

No sooner than I had sent the text, my phone rang.

"Monday? Like, five days from now Monday?" he responded.

I giggled. "Yes, next Monday. I accepted a very generous offer today, and we will close Monday mid-day, so I will be on the road thereafter."

"Do you need any help packing? Actually, I never asked: how are you getting your stuff back East?"

"I am renting a small U-Haul trailer. In the end, I have about thirty boxes and no furniture, so the move shouldn't be too bad. I will pick up the trailer tomorrow and get my car outfitted with the hitch, etcetera, and start packing the trailer up on Friday through the weekend," I explained.

There was a pause, and then Hendrix asked, "May I stop by this weekend to say goodbye?"

An enormous smile crossed my face. "That would be really nice," I gushed.

"Sunday, around six p.m.?" he proposed. "I will bring dinner since you probably have nothing."

"Perfect."

"Great. It's a date, then. See you Sunday around six. Have a great night."

"You, as well." I hung up and rolled over in bed, grinning from ear-to-ear.

I wondered, when he had stated, "*It's a date*," did he really mean a date-date or something else. I tried not to think too hard about it. I was simply happy I would see him again before I left.

***

Thursday morning, Triniti arrived at my house at eight thirty on the dot. She and her friend packed the table chairs and some other small furniture pieces, like an end table and a side chair. Then we said our goodbyes and again promised to see each other on the island this summer.

Once they left, I headed over to U-Haul to get my trailer. Driving with a trailer was harder than they said it would be, but I managed.

When I got home, Colbie rang and said she and some friends could be over in the afternoon to take the bedroom furniture. I had been putting off packing my bedroom, as I didn't want to have to rummage through boxes every morning to get dressed, but now I needed to finish packing that up before this afternoon.

Now that I didn't have to worry about suits anymore, packing did go by rather quickly. In the back of my mind, I knew that I would need to buy more entrepreneur casual clothes, but it could wait.

I finished packing the bedroom then sat on the kitchen counter and ate my lunch, which consisted of celery, some Swiss cheese, and an apple. I had used up all my bread, so my go-to PB&H was off the menu.

Next thing I knew, my doorbell rang.

I answered the door for Colbie.

"We're here," she announced.

We hugged, and then she introduced her boys and a couple of other friends. I then led them upstairs to the bedroom and said, "Have at it."

In no time, they had the bed broken down. They carefully took the dressers and nightstands down the stairs, as I cautioned not to ding the walls. Within forty-five minutes, my bedroom was in the back of Colbie's truck. I stood in the driveway as they put the last piece in.

Colbie turned to me and said, "Thank you for this, Evie. I will always remember you as the person who reminded me to take care of myself. Be safe on your trip back East and call any time."

"Remember, my house is open any time you all want to come for a visit," I reminded her. I saw the boys give each other high-fives when they had heard that, which made me smile.

As they drove away, I went back into the house, feeling a little melancholy. My life was now in these thirty plus boxes. I lay on the floor of the living room and stared at the ceiling. Boy, I hoped I knew what I was doing.

I then heard, *"Do you trust me?"*

Yes, I thought to myself.

"Do you trust yourself?"

Yes.

"We are one in the same. Know everything will work out, and it will."

I said out loud, "Everything will work out perfectly; I know it."

***

Friday morning, I had absolutely nothing in my refrigerator, so I went out to my local coffee shop and grabbed a muffin and a cup of coffee. I had a big day of cleaning, and Tatum would be stopping by to pick up the paintings.

When I got home, my first task was cleaning the oven. My head was deep in the oven, trying to get that cooked-on stuff off, when I heard, "Evie, are you in here?"

I scrambled, pushing myself out of the oven. Unfortunately, I lifted my head a little too early and smacked it on the top of the oven.

"Ouch!" I yelled. Immediately, I saw stars.

I gave myself a second then shook my head and called out, "I'm in the kitchen."

Tatum looked at me as I stood up, rubbing my head.

"Are you okay?" she asked.

"Sort of," I answered.

"Sorry to have startled you. I knocked, and the door was ajar, so I let myself in," she explained.

"No worries. I must have not closed it when I got back from breakfast. So, how are you?" I asked.

"I'm great. Waiting for this amazing artist I know to get settled and start painting again," she joked.

I laughed. "Well, it will be really soon. I head out on Monday."

"Amazing. Do you need any help?"

"No, thank you. I am all packed. All I need to do now is give it a once-over cleaning. I'm taking my time since I have all weekend to do it."

"Okay, if you change your mind, please let me know." Then she reached into her bag and pulled out two checks. "Here you go." She handed them to me.

I stared at them for a few seconds, almost not believing my eyes.

"I have been waiting for this for a long time," I whispered.

Tatum noticed that my eyes were tearing up and came over to give me a huge hug. "This is only the beginning, Evie. Know that you are incredibly talented, and this will be your life's work, if you so choose."

When we separated, I wiped my eyes. "Give me a sec, and I will get the paintings."

I ran into the studio and grabbed the two paintings. I looked at them one more time then carried them back to the kitchen. "All yours."

Tatum took the paintings and looked at them, too. She physically shivered and said, "Your work gives me goosebumps. Please call me from the road and let me know when you get to the island. I want to make sure that you are safe and sound."

"Thank you, I will."

We said our goodbyes, and then I electronically deposited the checks into my account. I was going to keep the physical checks so I could frame them.

Matt called me later that day to say we were all good to go for Monday at eleven. He texted me the directions to where we would sign the documents and reminded me to leave any extra set of keys on the counter.

***

Friday and Saturday, I cleaned all day, so when Sunday rolled around, I was exhausted. I hadn't been sleeping well, as I was on the floor, but I looked forward to today—date night with Hendrix.

The house was cleaned, and the trailer was packed but for my toiletries and some clothes. I really had nothing to do but wait for tonight.

I paced around an empty house, but I needed to do something, so I rummaged around in the trailer and found my paints. Then I drove down to the local art store and bought a canvas. If I had hours, I might as well use them to create something.

I set up outside, as I didn't want to make a mess in my clean house, and propped the canvas up against a tree. I sat on the ground and stared at the canvas, a warm sensation overcoming me. I felt energy tickling the top of my head. I knew exactly what to paint.

A few hours later, my painting was complete. I stepped back and smiled. "Perfect." Then I realized that the day had passed and I needed to clean up, pack up my paints, and get ready for dinner with Hendrix.

Right at six, I heard a car pull into my driveway. I looked at myself one more time in the bathroom mirror before I headed for the door.

He rang the doorbell right as I opened the door, surprising us both.

"Hendrix."

"Evie, you surprised me." He walked into the house and gave me one of his wonderful warm hugs.

I took the food bags and asked, "What's for dinner?"

"I figured, since you love poke so much that you would also enjoy Japanese."

"Nice. I love Japanese." I smiled.

In preparation for our dinner, I had put a blanket down in the living room, setting it with paper napkins and plastic cups.

He walked in and said, "I love what you've done with the place."

"Yes, I am into the minimalist look," I retorted.

We both laughed as we sat down to dinner.

The food was amazing. I didn't know if it was really that good or if it was because I had been eating the most random things. Either way, I was having a fantastic evening. Our conversation went from work to the pandemic to family.

"I really enjoyed meeting your sister. She is very sweet."

"Thanks. She is my kid sister. We didn't know of each other until she was almost a teenager. Our father was a"—he paused—"man about town, so I have a very age-diverse family. She was getting in trouble, so I wanted to make sure that she knew she had options and that one of them was me. She lived with me until she was eighteen and got through high school. From there, she got herself into college and now only stops by when she needs money, or her clothes washed.

"I saw you two talking. What was she saying? She didn't embarrass me, did she?" he asked.

"No, she only said wonderful things about you. You can tell she looks up to her older brother."

He smiled and blushed a little.

After dinner and the wonderful conversation, I got up and disappeared into the other room. When I returned, I had the painting behind my back.

"I wanted to give you something so that you will remember me," I told him.

"Evie, you didn't have to do that. You already gave me half of your furniture; what else could you possible give me?" he questioned.

"Close your eyes."

When he did, I admired his handsome face for a moment then held up the painting.

"Okay, open your eyes."

Hendrix just stood there, staring, not saying a word. I actually got nervous.

"Do ... Do you like it?" I stammered.

"Evie, this is spectacular. This is for me?"

"Yes. I painted it today, so it may have some wet spots. I call this *Hendrix's Hugs*. This is my interpretation of the feeling I get when you give me one of your big, warm hugs."

Hendrix just stared at me then the painting, and then I saw his eyes tear up a little.

"Evie, this is the kindest, most thoughtful gift anyone has ever given me." He wiped his eyes then took in the painting again. He leaned it against the wall and gave me the biggest, most loving hug that I had ever received, next to my grandmother. I didn't want to let go, and I got the sense that he didn't want it to end, either.

Finally, we separated, and then he held me by the shoulders and said, "Evie, I have always been attracted to you ... since we first met. But I was in a bad place, and you seemed terribly busy with work. When you called me to help you find a new job, I was elated that we were connecting again. Your trust in me to help with your spiritual journey was the cue that I needed to allow myself to have feelings for you. Now you are leaving, and all I can do is be happy for you. I hope that we can stay in touch. I love having you in my life."

I didn't know what to say. I just looked at him then went in for another hug, burying my face into his chest. When I finally pulled myself together, I pushed away and said, "Thank you. I didn't know what tonight was going to be like. I knew we were friends, but I didn't dare think further than that. To hear you say this makes me so happy and sad at the same time." We both knew that this was something that I had to do, and if it was meant to be, it would be.

It was getting late, and I had a big day tomorrow. Hendrix gave me the leftovers for breakfast and carefully picked up his painting. I followed him to his car, where we embraced one more time before he left. I promised to call him on my trip and to let him know that I made it safe and sound.

I floated back to the house where I fell onto the floor, just beaming with joy. What a night. Not only did he like my painting, but he liked me, as well.

***

Monday morning hit with a bang. I woke up startled, not knowing what time it was. I had actually fallen asleep rolled up in the blanket that we'd had our picnic on.

I grabbed my phone. Shit, it was nine a.m.

I ran upstairs, jumped in the shower, and then pulled on my most comfortable but nice clothes that I had left out. Once I was dressed, I packed the last of my clothes, blankets, and toiletries in an open box then brought it out to the trailer.

I grabbed the leftover Japanese food and nuked it for a few minutes. Then I took my breakfast and walked the house, making sure that I hadn't left anything behind. Everything looked great.

I put my extra set of keys on the kitchen counter, cleaned out the refrigerator of remaining condiments, and put it all in the garbage. Then I brushed my teeth, grabbed my bag and phone, and headed out to the car. I made sure that I had a mask for the closing. Things were definitely opening up, but there were still office building protocols.

I walked outside and closed the door to my house one last time. How symbolic. I was also closing the door to my old life. I smiled, knowing that there were so many more doors that were opening all around me.

I checked the trailer hitch on the U-Haul before I got into my car. And, as I was walking around, Sue came out of her house.

"Evie, I am really sorry to see you go, but I am very happy that you are doing something that you love," she said.

"Thanks, Sue. I truly appreciate that. I hope, on your journey, you also find your happiness. Remember to listen to your heart."

***

I got to the closing a few minutes early and met Matt outside.

"Are you ready?" he asked.

"Ready as I'll ever be."

The closing went as planned. I thanked Matt for all his help then checked my account to make sure the deposit had hit.

With a big smile, I got into my car and headed out to start the newest chapter of my life.

***

Four long days, nine states, a flat tire, horribly unhealthy food, and I finally arrived in Woods Hole. My boat reservation was at four, but I got there early and asked if I could get on an earlier boat, but I was told that there were no standbys. Therefore, I spun around and headed to the local grocery store in Falmouth to pick up a few things so I would have at least a little food in the house.

I got in line with an hour to spare, turned off the car, and closed my eyes. *In another two hours, I would be home,* I thought.

I must have fallen asleep, because the next thing I knew, I was hearing cars honking. They were already boarding. *Yikes.*

I turned the car on and slowly drove onto the boat. Luckily, they had me drive down the center, probably because they knew that I couldn't maneuver the trailer that well.

Once all the cars were loaded, I went upstairs to grab a chowder and a beer. It had been so long since I had been here that I didn't recognize what boat I was on. No matter. They still had beer, and that was what I needed.

I found a seat inside, next to the window, and watched as we pulled away. The ocean was so beautiful. The view was breathtaking.

I went out onto the deck and could feel my hair expanding as it soaked up all the moisture. I grabbed a tie out of my bag and quickly pulled my hair back so I didn't scare any of the animals or small children. Then I just sat out on the deck until I was beckoned by the loudspeakers for drivers to return to their vehicles.

This was the last leg of my trip. I was almost there.

As I sat in the car, waiting for my turn to unload, I felt an excitement come over me.

Finally, I was given the okay to start my car and drive off. I slowly exited the boat and, just like that, I turned into a child again, excited to see my grandparents.

Driving up island, even at dusk, I was overtaken by the beauty. Ocean, woods, brightly colored homes. I had forgotten how gorgeous this place was. Funny how I instinctively knew where I was going.

I finally reached my dirt road, turned in, and proceeded to hit every bump and hole, almost knocking the trailer off its hitch. *Need to work on that when I get some time*, I thought to myself.

I pulled up to the house, parked, and then walked up the overgrown shell driveway. At the door, I put in the key and, for a second, I swear I heard my grandmother calling my name. I opened the door and took a deep breath in. Musty but familiar.

I realized this was it. This was my happy place. This was home.

CHAPTER 10 — ISLAND GIRL

Even though it was dark, I slipped into the house, knowing exactly where to go. Unfortunately, I stepped on the infamous loose board, which created an annoyingly loud creak. I have long held the belief that it was my grandfather's homemade alarm system. He always denied it. It seemed like nothing had changed over all these years.

I flipped on a switch, but no light, so I hurried back to the car and got my flashlight out of the emergency kit.

As I reentered the house, the flashlight gave the room a warm but ominous feel. I was quickly transported back to being a teenager, hearing Grandma in the kitchen and Grandpa out in the yard. Spending time with my grandparents was always a double-edged sword. I loved being with them so much. They gave me stability and love, something that my mother was unable to do.

If I was visiting my grandparents, it meant that my mother was gone again. I never got a real explanation as to where she went, but she would always return, and we would go on with life. I had been sixteen when I'd heard the familiar, "We are going to visit your grandparents," and knew she would be gone again. That time, unfortunately, she never returned. All I remembered was Grandpa leaving the island, and when he returned, he had all of my stuff. We had never discussed it further.

I weaved through the house, assessing my surroundings. No electricity meant there was no water. I didn't want to look around too much and get overwhelmed with everything that needed to be done.

I checked my cell service. Okay, but not great. I still had seventy-five percent battery, so I was good for a day. I quickly sent a group text to Hendrix, Reva, and Colbie, letting them all know I arrived safe and sound. Then I turned off my phone to save my battery.

There was not much I could do tonight but try to get a good night's sleep. For whatever reason, I did not feel comfortable sleeping in the house, so I grabbed a pillow and blanket from the trunk of the car and got in the back seat.

Before I drifted off to sleep, I gave my appreciation to my higher self for getting me to the island safely. Then I looked at the night sky and forgot how dark it could get when there were no other lights around. The night was pitch black, yet the stars were so bright. It was an amazing night. What a magnificent way to start my new life.

***

When I woke, everything felt damp. I had left the windows slightly open, and the fog had rolled in. It was June, but the sun was just rising, and I was cold.

I looked around the car to see what I had to drink and eat. Half full bottle of water, bread, peanut butter, honey, some pork rinds, and beef jerky. No utensils, so I made a deconstructed PB&H sandwich by dipping the bread in honey and scooping it into the peanut butter. Then I grabbed the blanket and weaved around the side of the house to the back deck and ate my breakfast.

What a view. In the distance, to the left, was the lighthouse. To the right, I could see the ocean. Growing up, I hadn't appreciated the scenery of the island and the wonderful little enclave my grandparents had so painstakingly created.

The deck was creaky, but it seemed stable enough. I sat down and leaned up against the house, closed my eyes, and meditated, setting my intentions for the day.

The scent of saltwater roused me from my meditation. I missed that smell.

Not knowing what time it was, I shuffled back to the car, trying not to drag the blanket or get it tangled in the overgrown brush. I turned on my phone. Six thirty. Wow, it was still early.

I noticed that I didn't have great cell service, so I pivoted around in the driveway until I found the perfect spot that gave me at least four bars. Immediately, there were three texts that popped up. I smiled and checked Hendrix's first.

> *Evie, so happy you made it safe and sound. Every day since you left, I sit on my new couch, feeling your presence, and stare at your stunning painting. Miss you. Call when you can.*

Hmmm, even his texts are like a big, warm hug. Colbie's text was just as sweet.

> *Evie, congratulations on starting your new life! The boys and I are so proud of you. They are already scheming on when we can come and visit. I know you will be busy, so I will wait for you to call me. Take care.*

Reva's text was quintessential Reva.

> *Glad you made it. Make sure you eat and get enough rest. You can't clean everything in one day. Call me so I can plan my trip to come down and help. Love ya.*

Nice to know Reva was willing to help. Not like I doubted it for a moment.

Now, that the sun was up, I ventured into the house. First thing, I opened all the windows to let the air circulate and get out some of that musty smell. The spiders hadn't taken over too badly. As I continued to inspect, I noticed a nest of some kind, so I guessed I had a roommate.

There was really not a lot I could do without electricity, so I went into the bathroom, looked in the mirror, put on my ball cap, and checked my face to see that I didn't have any crud in my eyes. Then I went back outside and clumsily unhitch the U-Haul. Good thing I had been doing my yoga, or I really could have busted my poopa. I grinned, knowing that would be exactly what my grandmother would say.

My first stop was town hall so I could pick up my beach pass and to basically let people know I was in the house. Didn't need the town police coming over, thinking I was a squatter.

When I got to the town hall, I noticed how things still looked the same. Granted, there had been some updates, but no major overhauls.

I went to open the door when I notice the sign that required masks for entry. *Shoot.* I ran back to the car and grabbed one from the front seat.

When I greet the woman behind the window, she gave me a funny look. Finally, she said, "Ma'am, do you know that you have a big glob of peanut butter on your mask?"

I went completely red and started babbling about how I got in late last night, no water or electricity.

Her response was a halfhearted, "Uh-huh."

"I would like to pick up my beach pass. My name is Evie Prince."

"Oh, are you the family of Peter and Lilly Prince?" she questioned.

"Yes, I am their granddaughter."

I had forgotten how well known my grandparents were. My grandfather had worked in the boat yard, repairing and caring for other people's boats, and my grandmother had cleaned houses for the summer folk and was an artist for fun.

"So, how long are you here for?" she asked, as if I was just a summer dink.

"I am here permanently. Just moved from Colorado."

"Really? Well, welcome. So, what do you do?"

I paused then broadcast, "I'm an artist."

"Would I know your work?"

I smirked. "Not yet, but you will soon."

With that, she slid the beach pass to me, and then we said our goodbyes.

Now I needed to head down island to get my utilities set up and buy gas and groceries.

***

The drive down island was busier that I had expected, but then I remembered it was summer. I always recalled the island population growing five times over in the summer months, and it seemed like nothing had changed that.

As I approached Five Corners, I entered it with trepidation. It literally was five roads that converged. Then add pedestrians and if the ferry was unloading, you had a real cluster. You had to trust that people knew the rules of the road. Any slight hesitation, and you lost your turn. I made it through without issue then pulled into the closest gas station.

OMG! I couldn't believe the price of gas. Mental note: always fill up before coming to the island.

I steadily made my way to the electric company. It took me a while because of traffic and … I got lost. This time, however, I located a clean mask before entering the building.

I had no problem getting my utilities set up into my name. I was told that I should have power by the end of the day. Not exactly trusting the timeline, when I went to the market, I bought candles, an extra flashlight, and batteries. It was always good to have extras on hand. One good nor'eastern and the power was out. I also made sure to get a few extra-large bottles of water for drinking and washing up.

The trip down island took longer than expected, but it was enjoyable to explore the island again. Right before I headed up island, I took the opportunity to get some coffee and plug in so I could have a full charge on my phone.

While I waited, I closed my eyes and suddenly felt Hendrix. I needed to call him.

The phone rang a number of times before he picked up.

"Evie," Hendrix answered in a harried voice.

"Hi, Hendrix. Are you okay?"

"Uh, it's Nik. She is sick."

"What do you mean, she is sick?" I gulped.

"She had been staying with me, and she started to feel ill two days ago. We thought it was Covid, but her test came back negative. They don't know what's wrong with her. She is still in the hospital. The worst part is I can't be with her." His voice filled with concern.

"I am so sorry. Is there anything I can do for you?"

"You are doing it already. Hearing your voice just brings me peace. Thank you."

"Please keep me posted on how things are going. My cell service isn't great, so I will call when I can."

"Evie, I do have one request."

"Sure," I replied.

"Please send my sister healing energy."

"Of course. Hendrix, she will be okay. Stay strong," I encouraged.

"Hearing your voice helps keep me positive. Thank you," he whispered.

***

The entire drive back up island, I kept thinking of how to send Nik healing energy.

When I pulled into the dirt road, I saw the house from a new view. Coming in last night, I hadn't really seen the house. Now I saw it all in its rundown glory.

My grandparents had always kept this house so pristine. It is a two-bedroom, one and a half bath cottage. Grandpa had kept the garden and landscaping perfect, and Grandma had kept the house flawless. Now it was a shell of what it had been.

"Don't worry, Grandma and Grandpa; she will be beautiful again."

I sat in the car for a moment and closed my eyes before I went inside. I asked my higher self how to send healing energy to Nik.

As my mind cleared and I entered a meditative state, I heard, *"Think of her with love. Let your energy rise and think of her with love."*

To raise my energy, I thought about when I had met Nik—her beauty, easy-going personality, and how much she looked up to Hendrix. A wide smile crossed my face. Then I asked the Universe to send Nik my love.

I literally felt my heart rate increase. It was like a surge of energy came over me. Then I observed the energy leave me and visualized it going to her.

Wow, that was powerful, I thought. Never had I experienced something like that before.

I sat for a few more moments then grabbed my bags and brought them into the house. First thing first, I needed to clean the kitchen, bathroom, and my bedroom.

Winding through the house, I turned on a few lights so that I would know when the power came on. Then I turned the faucet on. Nothing. I had two large bottles of water. I would use one for cleaning and washing, and the other for drinking.

As I stood at the kitchen window, I saw someone walking through the backyard. Mr. Brown, a neighbor who I hadn't seen in years.

I knocked on the window and waved then headed outside.

"Evie, I heard you bought your grandparents' house. When did you arrive?"

"Hi, Mr. Brown. So nice to see you. I arrived late last night."

"Please, call me Attaquin. Since your grandfather died, I tried to check on the house every week or so to make sure nothing bad happened."

"No wonder things look so good. Thank you for taking such good care of the house for us. I mean, me."

"So, how long are you here for?"

"Indefinitely. I sold my house in Colorado."

"Congratulations. You are a smart girl." He grinned. "Well, let me know what you need. Some dinner maybe?"

"Thank you." I sighed. "That would be fantastic."

"Done. I went hogging the other day, so I have some fresh chowder and stuffers."

"Yum. I'm there. What time?" I inquired.

"Five. I'm old, so I do the blue plate special." He chuckled.

I watched as Mr. Brown disappeared back through the bushes.

When I got back inside the house, I noticed it was brighter.

"Yes! I have power."

I had two hours before heading over for dinner. Time to clean.

I turned on the kitchen faucet. *Clank, clank, sputter*, and finally, brown water started flowing out. I let the water run for a while until it became clear. Nice, now I had water and power. What more could a girl ask for?

I went into the bathroom, off the main bedroom, and decided this was my first target. Not as bad as I expected, but it was no walk in the park, either. After an hour of detailed cleaning, I now felt safe to use the bathroom. I then moved to my grandparents' room, which I guessed would now be my bedroom.

I was uncomfortable cleaning this room because it had so many personal items. My grandparents had been private people, and there was so much that I didn't know about them. Just being in here made me feel like I was intruding. Therefore, I decided to move to my old room, even though it only had a single bed. I was fine sleeping in there for the time being.

I looked at my phone and saw that I only had ten minutes before my dinner with Mr. Brown. Not much I could do with myself other than retie my hair and put on a clean sweatshirt. I then followed the worn path through the bushes over to Mr. Brown's house.

Attaquin Brown was a member of the local indigenous tribe and had been a fisherman for as long as I had known him. He and my grandfather had been the best of friends. I remembered many nights, when I was already in bed and would hear them out back, telling fishing stories and hearing about the ins-and-outs of island life.

"No need to knock. Come on in. You are just in time," Attaquin said when he saw me through the screen door.

"Mmm … dinner smells wonderful. I am starving."

"Well, that's good. Got plenty."

I sat down at the kitchen table as Mr. Brown brought over a big bowl of chowder and opened a fresh bag of soup crackers.

"Can I get you something to drink? I got water and a couple of beers. What's your poison?"

"Ooo … I'll take a beer. Nothing better than beer and chowder."

We sat in silence, enjoying the chowder. It felt like I hadn't had a real meal in a long time. Mr. Brown always made the best chowder, too. Not too thick and always filled with quahogs. My grandmother used to try relentlessly to get his recipe, but he would never divulge his secret.

"Mr. Brown, this seems even better than I remembered. Did you ever give Grandma your recipe?"

He looked up from his bowl. "Not on your life." He laughed. "So, what brings you back. Must be something big, leaving the city and your important job to come live here. So, what happened?"

Mr. Brown was the salt of the earth—practical, wise, didn't mix words, and always knew when something was up.

I took my last spoonful of chowder, a sip of beer, then started my sorted story. "Well, where to begin?" I told him about being laid off and my desire to paint again. I did not, however, tell him about my new spiritual realizations.

He looked at me sideways, probably knowing I was only telling half the story. "So, you gonna take up where your grandmother left off?"

"Huh? What do you mean?"

"You gonna be an artist and paint like your grandma?"

"I hope to be half as talented as her."

He looked at me as if he already knew and said, "Don't worry; you will create amazing art. Now, do you have enough room for a stuffer?"

"Always."

After another hour of small talk, I headed back through the bushes. Mr. Brown said he would come over tomorrow to make sure the stove worked and to get the refrigerator running.

The sun was just about set and the sky was filled with vibrant reds, orange, and yellows. I sat on the back deck, watching until the sun disappeared. Then I rummaged through the trailer, looking for the linen closet boxes before I headed back into the house. The sheets were too big for the single bed, but they were clean.

I had traveled so much through my life that sleeping in a new place normally didn't bother me but, for some reason, I was not comfortable in the house, not yet at least. It was too quiet. I left a few lights on just to give me some comfort and to keep any animals away. Then, before I headed to bed, I sent Hendrix a text, asking how Nik was doing and telling him about my day. Sleep came quickly.

CHAPTER 11 — WEED?

When I woke, I recalled a strange dream. All I had heard was, *"Protect yourself."* What did that mean?

I got out of bed and walked outside to feel the day. It was already feeling warm, so it was going to be a hot one. I went back in to put on some shorts, a T-shirt, and my ball cap, ready for a new day of cleaning. Before I started in earnest, though, I saw Mr. Brown walking through the yard with two cups of coffee. I met him outside.

"Slept in late. Must've been tired."

"Really? What time is it?"

"Oh, it's nearly seven. Need some coffee? Black."

"Yes, thank you." I took a sip. "Whoa, this will keep me going all day."

"Ready for me to check your stove?"

"Sure."

As I watched him work, I saw Hendrix had replied to my text.

Evie, so wonderful to get your text. You know exactly when I need—your energy. Nik is still in the hospital. They think it is a viral infection, and she is on some heavy antibiotics. If she responds well, she could be home in a few days. Yesterday, she told me that she felt a wonderful peace come over her, then she thought of you. Thank you for

*sending her your healing energy. It obviously
helped. If you don't mind, I will try to call you
later today.*

I looked at the phone, amazed. "It worked ..."

Mr. Brown looked over his glasses at me and asked, "What did you say?"

"Oh, nothing. I was just thinking out loud."

"Everything okay last night? I noticed you had your lights on all night."

"Yeah, kind of. I just wasn't comfortable. Plus, I found a nest in my grandparents' room, and I wanted the animals to know I live here now."

"What's up? This is your house. Your *family's* house."

"I know, but ... I feel like I am intruding. Since I moved out to Colorado, I didn't come back too much. Plus, Grandpa was always so private," I explained, trailing off.

"Do you want me to smudge the house?"

"Do what?" I exclaimed.

"Purify the house."

"Oh ... Please, that would be fantastic!"

After he checked the stove and plugged in the refrigerator, he went back to his house. Within a few minutes, he was back with a large shell, filled with something. I watched him light it then fan the smoke. He slowly walked around the exterior of the house, moving the smoke and whispering something. Then he came inside. It smelled like weed. He moved through each room, making sure that the smoke reached every corner.

When he was done, I looked at him and questioned, "Weed?"

He gave me a funny look. "No. Sage. You should be all set. Whatever energies you were feeling should be cleared out."

Did he say energies? I wondered.

***

For the rest of the day, I was nonstop cleaning. The bathroom was done, but I had to get the kitchen finished so that I wouldn't have to rely on Mr. Brown to feed me. The refrigerator was the hardest part. Boy, this was going to be a heavy-duty dump run.

The dump was open Tuesday, Thursday, and Sundays in the summer. If you had time to chat, you could always find out what was going on in town if you talked to the attendant. You also might find something to take home.

On the side of the attendant building there was a table where people could put gently used items for someone else to take. After going through this house, I was convinced that I would be large contributor to the dumptique.

It was late afternoon, and I was physically done. I rested against the house on the back deck. My body ached, but it had felt good doing manual labor. I glanced at my phone and realized that I had a text; Hendrix asking if I had time to chat. I immediately dialed his number.

"Evie?"

"Hey, Hendrix. How are you?"

"It is so good to hear your voice. Thanks for calling."

"How is Nik?" My voice was filled with concern.

"She is responding to the meds, so she should be home in a couple of day."

"That's fantastic news!" I squealed

"Yes, we are both very relieved. So, are you getting settled?"

"Yes, bit by bit. An old friend of my grandparents', who was also their neighbor, has been helping me a lot. He actually smudged the house."

"Nice. Is this the first time you experienced that?"

"Yeah. I didn't understand why he was burning *weed* and walking around the house. I quickly learned it was sage."

Hendrix busted out laughing. "Yes, I guess you are right; it does smell similar. Well, I'm glad that you are being cared for. I will need to thank your neighbor when I see him."

Hendrix's comment made my heart flutter.

"Oh, so are you planning a vacation soon," I inquired coyly.

"Actually, I was hoping in August. I have this artist friend, who I am extremely fond of, and she just moved out East. My plan is to see her."

"Really? She sounds special."

"She is. Beautiful inside and out. Believes in herself so much that she took an amazing leap of faith. Her light shines brightly, and her loving energy is strong. Yeah, I would say she was special."

There was a pregnant pause, as I didn't know what to say to that.

"Well, I look forward to meeting her."

We closed the call by agreeing to speak daily. I realized at that moment that I was starting a relationship.

"You hungry? Blue plate special ready in fifteen minutes." I heard Mr. Brown yell through the bushes.

I laughed then yelled back. "Do I need a reservation?"

"Nope, first come first served," he responded.

I went inside to wash up and try to make myself presentable, and then, as I poked through the bushes, I could smell fish being cooked on the grill. My mouth watered. Mr. Brown was at the grill, tending to two beautiful slabs of fish.

"Just caught today. Blue and a fluke."

I could eat fish every day, and Mr. Brown might be the one to make that wish come true.

"Go inside and get yourself something to drink. I'll be right in."

I headed inside and went to the refrigerator. He had restocked the beer, so I grabbed one. Then I ran over to open the screen door when I saw him trying to balance the tray in one hand and the grill tools in the other.

He placed the tray on the table then grabbed an already prepared salad from the fridge. Lastly, he pulled some cornbread from the oven.

"Mmm … everything smells so good."

"It's nothing."

But I knew differently. It seemed Mr. Brown was enjoying having a neighbor again.

"You were busy today," I commented.

"When I left you, I had a feeling the fish would be running, so I went out for a bit."

"You also had time to go down island? I saw you restocked the refreshments, too."

"Nah, they deliver. I don't go down into that mess unless I have to."

"Well, I need to go tomorrow. Now that the refrigerator is cleaned and working, I need food. Can't expect you to feed me every night."

"It's been nice having the company, so you are welcome any time."

Tonight's dinner was equally as good as last night's. Reva would be proud that I was eating.

"Do you need me to pick you up anything while I'm down there?"

"Nope, I am good for the time being."

After a delicious dinner, we sat outside and enjoyed the sunset.

"Well, I better head out. Tomorrow is an early day. Thank you, as always, for taking care of me."

Attaquin tipped his beer can at me. "My pleasure."

When I slipped through the bushes, I realized how dark it was, as I had forgotten to leave the outside light on. I didn't want to bother Mr. Brown, so I cautiously felt my way back, one foot in front of the other, like I was on a newly frozen pond, trying to assess if it was safe. Eventually, my eyes adjusted to the darkness, and I made it to the house with limited scratches.

Tonight was the first night that I felt comfortable in the house. I needed to remember to ask Mr. Brown about smudging and what exactly he had been saying.

After a greatly needed shower, I sat on the couch and closed my eyes, thanking my higher self for another wonderful day. I then heard, *"There are many energies in this house. Protect yourself."*

"Am I in danger?" I whispered.

"No, do not worry. Protect yourself until you are prepared to learn more about your family."

My eyes popped open. "What does that mean?"

Feeling anxious now, I got ready then crawled into my single bed. *Protect myself* kept on running through my mind. How would I do that, and what was I going to learn about my family? I decided to call Colbie tomorrow to see if she could explain.

***

At the crack of dawn, I got ready to head down island. This was going to be a big shopping trip, so I put a cooler in the trunk to keep everything chilled for the trip back up island. Before shopping, I stopped by a little coffee shop to grab breakfast—coffee and a ham and cheese croissant. Still as good as I remember.

Each town I entered, I could feel the change in energy—more people and cars. I couldn't tell if it was me projecting, or me feeling everyone else's energy. Either way, I was making this trip as quick as possible.

I focused my positive energy on finding a parking space and having an enjoyable experience and, just as I pulled into the store's parking lot, someone pulled out from a spot up front.

"Nice. Thank you!" I exclaimed.

One hour and two hundred and fifty dollars later, I had completed my shopping mission. Because my grandparents had always done the shopping, I had never had to experience it firsthand. I recalled them always grumbling, and now I completely understood. The day trippers were in the snack and drink aisles, the summer dinks lollygagged, and the islanders were bobbing and weaving through them all, only acknowledging other islanders along the way. It truly was a sight to see. I was simply happy to be loading the last of my groceries into the trunk, so I could get back to the quiet of up island.

Just as I was about to close the trunk, I heard someone call my name.

"Evie? Evie Prince, is that you?"

I looked up to see my high school math teacher, Mr. Frank, standing next to my car.

After my mother had died, I had attended Martha's Vineyard Regional High School for my junior and senior years. Mr. Frank was a good man. He had known I had been going through and took me under his wing.

"Mr. Frank?"

"Yup, one in the same. How are you doing, kid?"

"I'm great."

"Here for the summer?"

"Actually, I just moved back from out West. "

"Really? Were you in California? I always thought you would live there."

"No, Colorado."

"Well, welcome back. Living at your grandparents'?"

"Yes, just arrived a few days ago."

"You look great. Colorado treated you well."

"Aw … thanks."

"Well, I won't keep you. I'm sure I will see you again when the summer is over." He smirked.

***

Forty-five minutes later, I pulled onto the dirt road, trying to avoid the bumps and holes. Those darn tourists. Not knowing where they were going, driving too slow, and always with an indicator blinking, so you never knew if they were really turning or not.

Geez, I sounded like an islander already and I hadn't been here a week.

I did better driving the dirt road this time than my first night here, but I had to get this road fixed, or I would lose my muffler.

I unpacked the groceries, wiped them down, and then put everything away. When I opened the fridge, there was a nicely wrapped piece of fish.

Mr. Brown, love that man.

I flopped down on the couch and rested my feet on the coffee table. If my grandmother saw me do that, she would have had my head.

I looked up and said, "Sorry, Grandma," with a cheeky smile.

Before I continued my quest of a clean house, I called Colbie to see if she could help me get clarity on my message to protect myself. The phone rang a number of times, and I was getting ready to leave a message, when I heard, "Evie, give me a sec."

"Okay."

A few minutes later, Colbie returned to the phone.

"Sorry about that. I was booking a client on the other line, but I didn't want to lose you," she explained.

"Client? What do you mean, *client*?"

"Well ... I have started my own business. A healing business."

"What do you mean, *healing business*?"

"Just that I help to heal people spiritually. I have been working on this for a while, but it wasn't viable until just a few weeks ago."

"Wait—you had been working on this while I was still there, and you didn't tell me?"

"I gave you a hint that I had something in the hopper, but I didn't want to speak before it was time."

"Congratulations! That is brilliant news. And you already have clients?"

"I have been doing this on the side for a few years, but it wasn't formal. Now it is official with a name and business cards."

"So, what is the name?"

"Energy Works"

"I am so happy for you. You have definitely found your calling. I can attest that you have been helping me heal through this life change, so if you need references, just let me know."

"Thanks. I may take you up on that. So, how is it living back on the island?"

"It really is a big change from Colorado, but I am loving it!" I exclaimed "My grandparents' good friend and neighbor has been a huge help and wonderful company. He even smudged my house."

"Hmm ... why was that necessary?" Colbie probed.

"Well, that is partly why I am calling. I haven't told you much about my upbringing, but my mother died when I was a teenager. She was constantly leaving to go who knows where and, when that happened, I stayed with my grandparents. The last time she left me was when I was sixteen. She didn't return. My grandparents didn't tell me anything. Life just went on.

"My first night on the island, I slept in the car. I just didn't feel comfortable in the house. Mr. Brown, my neighbor, said he would smudge the house. It worked. But then, in my meditation yesterday, I was told to protect myself until I was prepared to learn more about my family."

"Wow, that's a pretty big message."

"Right? What do I do with something like that?"

"Have you ever heard of mediums?"

"Yes. Aren't there TV shows about them?"

"Well, yes, but we all have the ability to speak with people who have left this physical world, if you open up to it. The issue is, when you open up, you need to protect yourself from other energies that may want to attach to you."

"Colbie, this is starting to freak me out now."

"There is nothing to worry about. This may give you the answers you are seeking that you are not aware of yet. I will teach you how to protect yourself so, when you are ready, you can engage with the energies safely."

"Do you protect yourself?"

"All the time. It is very important in healing work, as I don't want to take on someone else's energy."

"Okay, what do I need to do?"

"First, close your eyes. Take some deep breaths. Now visualize a beautiful, bright white light. This light can be an orb or simply rays of light. Once you see the light, visualize yourself walking into that light. You are now completely surrounded by the white light. This light is your protection. Only love and positive thoughts can reach you through this light. Negative thoughts or energy may not penetrate this light ... Good. Now open your eyes. How do you feel?"

"I had a little difficulty visualizing the light, but once I got it, it felt so warm and comforting. But, that's it?"

"Yup. It may seem simple, but it is enormously powerful. The clearer you can visualize the light and you in it, the more powerful it becomes. You can do this every day, or at different times during your day. I would suggest that you protect yourself before going to bed and again in the morning."

"Colbie, this is so amazing. I would never have known how to do this myself. Thank you."

"No problem. I would hazard a guess that your neighbor may also have information that could help you. Not everyone smudges."

She raised a good point.

Colbie and I talked a little longer before hanging up. It was always such an enlightening experience when I spent time with her.

Before I went back to cleaning, I then texted both Tatum and Triniti to let them know that I made it safely. My last indulgence before cleaning was to call Hendrix. I just wanted to hear his voice. Unfortunately, the call went directly to voicemail.

"Hi, Hendrix. It's Evie. Just wanted to hear your voice. Call me when you can."

Today's task was to completely empty out the U-Haul so I could return it. Over the past few days, I had been relocating the boxes from the trailer to the house. Today, though, I would complete the task. I would just put it all in my grandparents' room.

I rearranged some furniture and carefully pushed their bed against the wall to make a larger walkway. Moving the bed exposed an old footlocker. It was locked, so I just slid it back under the bed, knowing I would need to deal with that later. With some strategic placement, I was able to get every last box into their room.

CHAPTER 12 — THE KEY

The house was finally feeling like my own.

Prior to bringing all my grandfather's clothes to the thrift store, I called over to Mr. Brown to see if he wanted anything.

"Thanks for asking, Evie. There is one item that I have always been fond of—his oil skin jacket."

"Of course. Take it. It's yours." I happily handed it over to him.

Mr. Brown held it carefully in his hands for a few minutes, as if contemplating. Then he looked at me and said, "Do you know how proud your grandfather was of you?"

I blushed, but held eye contact with Mr. Brown as I said, "Actually, no, I don't know. He never told me."

"Well, you know that wasn't his way."

"That may be true, but he was clear as day when he said to give up painting and get a real job. Hearing him say that broke my heart. That was a gift that Grandma had given to me, and he wanted me to give it up," I replied with tears in my eyes.

"He knew he hurt you, but he was just protecting you."

"From what?" I demanded.

"He didn't want you to end up like your mother."

"What? Dead? I am really trying to not be disrespectful, but what right did he have? I know absolutely nothing about my mother or how she died. I don't know who my father is and barely know anything about my grandparents. Everyone just left me in the dark to fend for myself." I unknowingly raised my voice. "Do you know what that does to a teenager? I gave up the love of painting to please my grandfather. Then I worked hard, like he said, sticking to what I know. But, did he ever say he was proud? Let me answer that for you. No, he didn't!" I screamed. "Now, I am supposed to believe that he was proud and that he broke my heart to protect me?" I stopped to take a few deep breaths. "Mr. Brown, I am having a hard time understanding all of this, and I am trying not to take it out on you."

"Evie, there is a lot that you don't know. I am not one to judge whether or not your grandparents managed it all properly, but you have to understand that they lost their only daughter, and they wanted to make sure that they cared for you in the best way they knew how.

"There is a lot that you will discover as you continue to go through the house. If you ever have questions, don't hesitate to ask. Your grandfather and I were best friends for a very long time. I am here to help you. I always have been, and I always will be. I made him that promise." With that, Mr. Brown walked out and quietly closed the door.

Right there, in the exact spot I was standing, I broke down, absolutely sobbing. So many questions, so many secrets. *Who am I? Who was my mother? Why did I suddenly feel so alone?*

My knees buckled, and I melted to the floor in a puddle of tears.

***

I didn't even know how much time had passed when I slowly opened my eyes to the sound of my phone..

"Hello," I answered with a soft, dry, scratchy voice.

"Evie, are you okay?"

I didn't answer immediately, finally saying, "I will be."

"Wh-what does that mean?" Hendrix stammered.

"I came back to start a new life, but I am realizing that, before I can do that, I need to learn about my family's lives so that I can finally become my own person and not who they thought I should be."

"Evie ... just remember you are strong. This is your life, don't let your family's lives and their decisions change how you want to live yours."

"Thank you, Hendrix. I needed to hear that. There are so many secrets, or just things that I was not told, that really influenced how my grandparents raised me. I try to remember that they did what they thought was best for me, but they didn't realize how their decisions impacted me."

Hendrix took a deep breath "Please remember that fear is based in love. Knowing that will help you see more clearly." I tilted my head to the side. "I'm not following."

"People act certain ways out of fear. They are afraid of losing something that they love, be it lifestyle, money, fame, family, love, health. It can be anything. They do the things they do to protect what they love. You may not agree but, to them, it was the only way they knew how to protect the one thing they loved. Look at everything through the lens of love. You may not forgive, but you will at least understand."

"I know this may sound silly, but can I have one of your hugs? I really need one right now."

"Happy to oblige."

At that moment, a warm feeling came over me. It was so peaceful and loving, and it was exactly what I needed.

"Thank you!"

"No, thank you. I will check in on you in the morning. Have a good night's sleep. Good night," he whispered.

"Good night," I replied.

***

I was out of the house early, trying to clear brush from the deck and around the house before the day started heating up. I could hear Mr. Brown next door, so I peeked through the bushes to say good morning.

"You're up early this morning," he greeted.

"Yup. Trying to beat the heat. I just wanted to come over and apologize. I felt horrible that I lashed out at you."

"No apologies needed. I know your words were not meant for me," he brushed it off. "I have some free time today; do you need some help?"

"I would love some. I don't remember how my grandfather kept the garden, so I am apprehensive about just cutting everything down."

"Evie, this is your house now; don't try to make it what it used to be. Make it what *you* want it to be."

"That's a great point, and you are the second person to say it to me. It's time for me to hear it and live it."

As we worked side by side, I felt like how I used to when I was young, helping my grandfather care for the garden. He'd had flowers, vegetables, and herbs. He would always have a table out at the end of the road with extras. He would just put a can out there and ask people to pay what they had for what they took. Sometimes, he would make money; other times, he would not. All he knew was that he was helping his neighbors who might not be as fortunate as him.

"Mr. Brown, can I ask you something?"

"Sure. What's up?"

"When you smudged the house … what did you exactly do?"

"I was cleansing the energy around and in your house. I asked the Great Spirit to remove any negative energy and to replace it with positive. As the smoke from the sage lifted, it took my prayers up to the Universe, creating a connection between our physical existence and the non-physical."

I was silent for a while. Then I finally mentioned, "I am just learning about spirituality."

"What do you mean, *you are just learning*? This is something that is innate in all of us. We are all spiritual beings," he said somewhat impatiently.

"I guess I should rephrase. I am just *remembering* and acknowledging that I am a spiritual being."

"Good!" Mr. Brown boomed. "All you need to do is be quiet and listen to nature. It will tell you everything that you need to know. That is how I have always lived my life, and my ancestors before me. The animals, from the fish to the hawk, to the creepy crawlies, know how to live a present life. The trees, the ocean, and with winds give us lessons every day. Appreciate them, and they will share their wisdom with you always."

"Mr. Brown, do you ever hear voices?" I questioned.

"Yes, it is one of the many ways that the Great Spirit communicates with us."

"Is the Great Spirit within you?"

Mr. Brown softened. "Yes. We are all one. The Great Spirit is within all of us, and we are all within the Great Spirit." That said, he turned back and continued to work.

We called it a day around eleven. I invited Mr. Brown in for an early lunch, and we laughed and reminisced about the time that I got caught trying to sneak back into the house after curfew. I had thought I was being slick, but I had ended up going through a burr bush and had to wake my grandparents to help me remove them from my hair and clothes.

Just before he left, he asked, "I suppose you stumbled upon the footlocker in your grandparents' room?"

"Yes, but it was locked."

He handed me a key. "Your grandfather asked that I give this to you when the time was right."

I took the key, passing it back and forth between my fingers. I knew that this would answer many of my questions.

I looked at him, teary-eyed, and mouthed, *"Thank you."*

***

"Girl, you better call me. I haven't heard from you in over a week."

I read the text, put down my coffee, and called Reva.

"Good morning."

"Uh-huh."

"Oh, don't be mad at me. Things have not been what I had expected," I explained.

"Well, tell me. What is going on, and how soon do I need to be there?" she questioned.

"Give me another couple of weeks. I still have to clean out my grandparents' room. Then I will have a proper place for you to sleep."

"So, where are you staying now?"

"In my old room," I murmured.

"Sounds like there is a story behind this. What is it?"

"I can't bring myself to sleep in their room. I feel like I am intruding. Plus, I am storing all of my stuff in there until I can get it unpacked." I continued, "I would like to have an estate sale, and I could definitely use your help getting ready for that."

"Sure. I could be there in a couple of weeks. Just keep me posted. So, what else is happening?"

"Just a bunch of emotional stuff. Being back here reminds me of things that I tried to get rid of. Things that I didn't understand or didn't really want to know. Now I have to face them all."

"Evie, just remember to give yourself some grace. Family issues always run deep, and for many, it takes their whole life to sort through them. Don't expect to have everything understood in two weeks. Take your time. They had a lifetime before you came into the picture, but it was their life," Reva reminded me.

"Yes, I know. Thank you."

We closed the call with me promising that I would call her every week, just so she knew I was okay.

I took a deep breath in and let it all out. Then I did my protection visualization and asked my higher self for grace as I learned about my family history. That done, I took the key from the kitchen windowsill and headed into my grandparents' room.

After moving a number of boxes, I finally reached under the bed to pull out the footlocker. It was heavier than I'd thought it would be. I dragged it out and into the living room, sitting on the floor, just staring at it. What could be in here? How would this change my life?

I took the key, gently placed it into the lock, and turned. When I opened the locker, I was stunned by the number of items that were in the locker. Everything was neat and organized. It contained photos, clothes, toys, newspaper clippings, and something wrapped in a brown paper bag. I ran my fingers gently over the items, trying to determine where to start. I landed on a photo with scalloped edges—a picture of my grandparents and a small child. I turned it over and, in pencil, was written: "*Ava, Lilly, and Peter 1964.*" As I flipped through the photos, I found more of my mother from elementary school, high school, birthday parties, out fishing, working in the garden … Many of them showed my grandfather, smiling and laughing with my mother. There was a beautiful picture of my grandmother showing my mother how to paint, just like she used to show me. I got the sense that my mother had a happy childhood.

When I lifted out all the photos, there was a stack of postcards wrapped in ribbon. Some dated back to 1985, and then as recently as 1996. They were mostly from South America. I flipped one over.

> *Hi, Mom and Dad.*
> *Made it safe and sound. We have already broke ground on the school, and the team should have it completed within another couple of weeks. Give my love to Evie.*
> *Love,*
> *Ava.*

I looked through a number of other postcards. All had similar messages—my mother helping build schools, teach children, helping mothers all throughout South America. Why had she never told me? Why had this been such a secret? Then I found the last postcard dated May 1996.

> *Hi, Mom and Dad.*

Things are getting a little hairy here. They have us laying low because the drug cartel is not happy that we are trying to provide education to the women and children of the village. The organizers are trying to get us out in the next few days. I will see you soon.
Give Evie a big hug and kiss for me.
I love you.
Ava.

I sat there, in complete silence, consumed with emotion.

My mother never made it back. She cared for others more than she cared for me, and I was the one who had lost out. How could she leave me, and why had my grandparents covered for her all this time?

My eyes started to fill with tears. I was mad at all of them, but I was also proud that my mother had risked her life to help others.

I went outside to get some air and to just decompress in the sun, but then I heard Mr. Brown next door and couldn't help my curiosity. I needed to find out what he knew.

Poking my head through the bushes, I must have startled Mr. Brown, as he jumped when I said hello.

"Geez, kid, what are you trying to do? Give an old man a heart attack?"

"Sorry, Mr. Brown, I didn't mean to scare you."

He looked at me, his face turning to concern. "What's wrong?"

"I opened the trunk and read the postcards. Why didn't anyone ever tell me? Why was it such a secret?" I questioned.

"Your mother was a free spirit and always wanted to help people. Your grandparents knew they couldn't stop her, so they agreed to take care of you when she was gone with the promise that she would never tell you what she was doing. They knew her work was dangerous, and they didn't want you to follow in her footsteps." He paused to study me. "Are you okay?"

"I don't know ... How could she leave her own child to help other children? What about me?"

"She knew that you would always be cared for ... better than she could ever do. She was not one to be tied down."

"So, I was an accident?"

"She was a young women who was filled with passion."

"So, I was a result of a one-night stand?"

"Evie, your mother loved you dearly. She was so proud of you. How smart and beautiful you were. But she was also fearful that you would want to be like her, and that was something that she could not allow. She struggled leaving you, but she believed that the women and children in South America needed her more."

"Thank you, Mr. Brown." I turned and walked back through the bushes.

Once inside the house, I closed the trunk, locked it, and then slid it into the corner of the room. I found myself saying, "I am not ready for this," and put the key back on the windowsill.

CHAPTER 13 — ME

Learning about my mother really took a toll on me. I didn't want to talk to anyone nor see anyone, and that included Mr. Brown.

It was late in the day when I got the impulse to feel the ocean. I slipped into my bathing suit, grabbed a towel, and went to the closest town beach. All the families had left for the day, so it was just a few couples who remained.

I dropped my towel, took off my shoes, and then walked to the water's edge. The sand was cool and felt refreshing on my feet. I had been so busy with the house that this was the first swim since I had been on the island.

I threw my clothes up by my towel then waded into the water. Yup, it was cold, but it felt good. I learned early on in life to just rip off the Band-Aid and jump in. Otherwise, it would take forever to get used to the temperature. Ah ... salt water.

I floated like a buoy. I was never a great swimmer, but I was definitely more buoyant in salt water than fresh or chlorine. I flipped on my back and just floated. It was so relaxing. It felt like the unrest that I'd had before just dissipated when I plunged into the ocean.

I heard the muffled sounds of the water as only my eyes, nose, and mouth were exposed. These sounds lulled me into a peaceful meditative state as I floated using my hands to steer me if I went out too far.

As I looked up at the sky, I heard, "*Paint, Evie. Paint your feelings.*"

That seemed like such a foreign concept. I had moved here, to the island, to paint, but so much had happened within the month that I had been here that I hadn't even thought about lifting a brush.

I stayed in the water a little longer then slowly walked out, not wanting to leave, but the sun was getting low and the mosquitos would soon be out in force. I wrapped the towel around my body, knocked off as much sand as I could from my feet, and then walked back to the car.

As I pulled out of the parking spot, I looked toward the lighthouse, seeing the two reds and a white of light. That lighthouse had kept me sane many a nights when I just hadn't known what to do after my mother's death. Nothing to think about; just red, red, white. A broad smile appeared on my face.

Entering the house, I felt renewed. I had a new confidence that made me feel like I could manage these rollercoaster feelings. I showered, dressed, found Grandma's easel, and got my paints out. I set myself up in the living room, placing a fresh canvas on the easel then closing my eyes. Emotions started to rise in me—sadness, anger, confusion, fear, loneliness. I allowed myself to feel it all then picked up my brush and started to paint.

Tears streamed down my face as I painted and painted. At times, my hands shook. Then I would yell, followed by uncontrollable crying. What resulted was a painting unlike anything else that I had ever painted. It was dark and gloomy. Dull colors, like blacks, greys, bloodred, and dark greens, in strokes that were jagged, sharp, and messy. Then a gradual transition had happened. My strokes were more fluid, lighter. Those same colors emanated a new radiancy until everything culminated into whiteness.

I dropped my brush and fell to my hands and knees. My breaths were deep and heavy. It felt like I had just run ten miles, and I was covered in sweat.

When I woke, I was curled up on the floor, shivering. It was night. There was only one light on that illuminated the painting. I looked at it. It was not beautiful. I didn't know what it was. Then I looked at it again.

It was me.

***

I heard a knock at the door and pushed myself from the floor seeing Mr. Brown through the window. I wrapped myself in the blanket and opened the door.

"Evie, are you okay?" Concern was written all over Mr. Brown's face. "I haven't seen you for a couple of days and—"

"I'm okay. Thank you for checking on me."

Mr. Brown grabbed my arm and sat me on the couch. Out of the corner of his eye, he saw my painting and froze.

"Evie ... this is ..." He stopped then finally said, "Phenomenal."

I hung my head and sat in silence.

After studying my painting for a time, Mr. Brown got busy in the kitchen, making me some coffee and scrambled eggs with toast. He brought it over and encouraged me to eat.

"I don't know if I can go on here ... in this house," I mumbled

"Evie, you need to give yourself some time. You just learned a lot of things and are experiencing a great deal of emotion. Just feel it, but remember, you are in control of how this information impacts your life."

"What do you mean?"

"Everyone loved you, and they did what they thought was best for *you*. You can take that information and try to see if from their point of view, and appreciate what they went through to make those decisions. Or, you can look at it from how you were impacted, stay mad, and feel cheated because your childhood was not like how it was *supposed* to be, or how you saw on television. You can be limited, or you can take this information and say thank you. Then go on and create the life that you choose to live. This is all up to you." He pushed the plate closer to me then quietly walked out.

***

After breakfast, I cleaned myself up then put away my paints and placed the painting on top of the footlocker. As I passed by the table to go outside, I accidentally knocked my phone to the floor and noticed that I had a number of missed calls and texts from Hendrix. I quickly dialed his number.

"Evie, is everything okay?"

"Yes," I said sheepishly. "I'm sorry that I have not called or responded to your messages. I have been dealing with a lot here, just learning about my mother, her death, and more about my grandparents."

"I am sorry, Evie. I did not know about your mother."

"Please, how could you? It's not something that I tell many people." I took a deep breath. "The long and short of it is that I lost my mother at the age of sixteen. She, unfortunately, did not return from one of her trips, and my grandparents never told me what happened. I found a footlocker that contained the particulars of my mother and my family, things I was never told. I have been trying to process it all and, as you say, *experience* life. Well, life has hit me so hard upside my head that I don't know if I have the strength to learn more." I sighed.

"You are strong, Evie. When I am in that place—and I have been there more times than I want to admit—I tell myself that this has already been solved, and I don't need to do anything else but follow my heart."

"Huh? You have lost me. What do you mean, *this has already been solved?*"

"All of the emotions you are experiencing are from things that have happened in the past. None of this is in the now, and it is not going to happen again in the future. Your higher self has infinite wisdom and knows what has happened, what is now, and what will happen. Your higher self has already solved this for you. Know that."

I didn't say anything for a few moments. Then I hesitantly sighed and said, "I guess."

"Just know that everything will work out, and it will," he said with finality.

"Well, if nothing else comes from this, I painted last night. The first time since I have been here. As I am learning, painting really helps me identify and process my feelings—good, bad, or otherwise. This painting reflects the otherwise. I call it *Me*."

"May I see it?"

"Sure." I took a picture then sent it to him via text.

I could tell when he received it, because I heard him mutter under his breath, "Whoa, this is intense."

"Now you can understand what I have been going through these past few days."

"Evie, sweetheart, take your time. There is no rush to learn it all. Just be and live your life. Enjoy the island. It's the summer. Stop worrying about what happened and enjoy what is now. That mindset will keep you sane. I speak from experience."

"Thank you for that. I so appreciate you," I told him then gasped. "In all of my anxiety, I forgot to ask about Nik. How is she doing?"

"She's good. Came home just the other day. Has been doing a lot of sleeping, but the doctors say she will make a full recovery. She really credits her healing to you."

"What? That is silly. You said that she was on antibiotics, so how could I have done anything?"

Hendrix paused and took a deep breath. "Evie, each one of us has the ability to heal ourselves and others. Nik was scared, and her anxiousness was causing her to not eat or sleep. The meds were doing nothing for her. When she felt you, she calmed down and knew that everything would be okay. That emotional shift allowed her body to take nourishment, rest, and allowed the medicines to do their jobs. Don't be shy about this gift you have. Your energy is powerful. Celebrate it."

I didn't know how to respond, so I just said, "May I have a hug?"

"Of course. This is the best part of my day—sharing this energy with you."

"Thank you. I can't wait for you to come and visit."

"I can't wait, either."

Before we hung up, Hendrix added, "Please don't ever scare me like that again. Evie, I truly care for you, and not knowing where you were, if you were okay, or how to get in touch with you had me out of my mind."

"I am sorry. It was not my intention." My voice was filled with sincerity. "Take this number. 508-645-9811. That is Mr. Brown's, my neighbor, number. He is the only person I see regularly and will know what is going on if you can't find me."

After we hung up, I sat there and reflected on what Hendrix had said to me. Was I a healer? Was my energy really powerful? I giggled

"He truly cares for me."

***

A few days past, and I finally decided to send a picture of my latest painting to Tatum.

> *Tatum,*
> *Hope you are well. Apologies for being MIA for so long. Lots of things to work through here.*
> *Attached is a photo of my latest work. I call it Me. Let me know what you think and if you may have a buyer.*
> *Look forward to hearing from you.*
> *Evie.*

Not long after, my phone rings. Expecting the call to be from Tatum, I was surprised to hear it was Triniti.

"Hello?"

"Evie, it's Triniti. How are you?"

"Triniti? Are you here?"

"Just got in last night."

"How long are you here for, and when can we see each other?"

"I will be here for two weeks, and I was hoping to get together tomorrow night. Dinner?"

"That would be great. I haven't really gotten out to see much of down island. So, to be shown around by a local would be fantastic," I said, tongue in cheek.

"Ha-ha. Let's meet at the Blue Duck Café at six."

"Sounds great. See you then."

I was really excited to see Triniti. It would be nice to have a friendly distraction. Also, I desperately needed to get out more.

***

Prior to heading down island to meet Triniti, I stopped by Mr. Brown's.

"Hello? Mr. Brown?"

"Back here," he yelled.

I walked around his house, weaving in-between lobster posts and nets. "Hi."

"Hey, kiddo. What's up?"

"I hope you don't mind, but I gave a friend your phone number in case of emergencies."

"That's fine. No worries at all. Heading into town?"

"How did you know?"

"You clean up good," he said with a chuckle.

"Thanks. Meeting a friend at the Blue Duck for dinner."

"From your high school days?"

"No, our paths actually crossed back in Denver. Come to find out, she grew up here on the island."

"What's her name? Maybe I know her family."

"I actually don't know. Her first name is Triniti."

"Well, she must be an islander because she knows the best place on the island to get lobster, next to catching it yourself. Be careful down there. Those summer people can be crazy."

"I'll watch myself. Have a great night."

The drive took a little longer because I got stuck behind a cyclist. The whole way down, I was already giving appreciation for the great parking space that I would get. There were people everywhere. You would not have known we had just been in a pandemic. The main street was packed!

I patiently drove to the end and, just as I was turning up a side street, a car pulled out. *Perfect timing.* I laughed.

When I arrived at the café, Triniti was already at the table. She greeted me with a big hug.

"Evie, so nice to see you. How was the drive?"

"I got caught behind a cyclist, but otherwise uneventful. It is so good to see you! How does it feel to be back home?"

"Great. My skin has moisture, but my hair … ugh!"

I laughed, knowing exactly what she was talking about.

She handed me a menu.

"I am told they have great lobster, is that true?" I probed.

"Yes. It's funny. Kind of a secret menu item. No frills. Boiled with a side of butter and a wedge of lemon."

"Isn't that the only way to eat it?" I remarked.

"Exactly! You just hope you get one. They use their own pots, so when the lobster is gone, it's gone."

The waiter greeted us while pouring two glasses of water. Just before he asked for our order, we both announced that we would like the lobster.

"Okay, that was easy. It's your lucky day; we still have some," he replied. "Any appetizers to start?"

Triniti looked at me and whispered, "If you like ice cream, there is a place down the street that makes it homemade, so save room."

We both looked up at the waiter and shook our heads.

When he walked away, we both busted out laughing.

It felt so nice to just be and enjoy the company. It seemed like I hadn't done this in a long time.

"Evie, so tell me, how was the drive?"

"Ugh. It was nice to see the country, but the food … not so much. I tried to pack as many healthy snacks as possible, but I couldn't wait for the drive to be over. Oh, I also got a flat tire."

"No! That is the worst. Did you fix it yourself?"

"I did. So proud of myself, but it was one of the scariest experiences. Cars whizzing by. Luckily, it was on the passenger side. The donut got me to a mechanic where I had to buy a new tire," I explained.

"I remember driving out with my ex-boyfriend. Unless you have the time and can really sightsee, I wouldn't want to do it again, and I can't imagine doing it by myself."

"Yup, been there, done that. Won't do it again," I noted.

"So, how is your new job? Things getting better?"

"Oh, yes. I really lucked out." She laughed then corrected herself. "I have created a great new life for myself, and your help was the icing on the cake."

I grinned at her. "So glad I could help."

"What about you? Painting?"

"Yes, I actually just finished one. Very different from my others," I admitted.

"Do you have a photo?"

I scrolled through my phone to find the picture that I had sent to Hendrix and Tatum then slid it over.

Triniti gazed at the photo then put the phone down and closed her eyes. She was quiet for a few seconds before she told me, "Evie, that painting is ... so heart-wrenchingly beautiful. The emotion is palpable. Are you okay?" She set her hand on mine.

Just before I could answer, the waiter set down two platters with bright red lobsters and corn.

"Enjoy, ladies."

We answered, "Thank you," in unison.

Then I turned back to Triniti and said, "I'm okay, but I will be better once I eat this delicious looking lobster." I smiled with the shell cracker in hand.

We both jumped into our meal, juice flying, butter dripping, and the shout of pride when I pulled the entire tail out of its shell.

"Mmm ... this is fantastic," I grunted as I finally looked up from my plate.

Triniti laughed and nodded in agreement.

I sat back in my seat and slowly picked through the lobster carcass to see what else I might find. Finally, I went for the little legs and suck out any deliciousness that might be left.

"So, you really are okay?" Triniti began.

"I am a work in progress. My entire life, there always seemed to be secrets or information that I was not given. Like, who my father is, where my mother went when she traveled, how she died. These questions caused me to always question myself. Was it my fault? Did I do something wrong? I always tried to please everyone else but myself. So, coming back here and cleaning out my grandparents' house, I am finding some of those answers and am desperately trying to process all of this in a nonjudgmental way," I admitted.

"I could feel the confusion and pain in your painting, but I could also see some clarity. You really are gifted," she complimented.

"Thank you, but I must say the same to you. I never really got the opportunity to compliment you on the vase that you gave me. I love it and have it prominently displayed in the house. I also painted a picture of that vase and the feelings I received when you gave it to me. It was such a joyful moment. So, thank you for sharing your gift of beauty with me."

"I love working in clay. I forgot what famous artist said this, but it is genuinely like there is something already in the clay and I am just exposing it. I wanted to give you something that expressed my gratitude. I was just coming out of a really bad place. My former relationship took everything. I had nothing, physically, mentally, or spiritually. When you gave me the desk chair, and then the bedroom *and* kitchen furniture, it helped me remember that there is still light in this world. That is what you are to me—you are a magnificent light."

We both smiled at each other then sat in silence until the waiter returned and asked if we wanted dessert.

"No, we are good," we said simultaneously then broke into laughter. It was like we were best friends from way back. Our connection was strong, and it was just easy to be myself with Triniti. There were only a few other people in this world that I'd had this easy rapport with, so I knew Triniti and I would remain friends.

We paid the bill then walked down the street, bobbing and weaving through all the tourists window shopping and reading menus. The ice cream shop was busy, but this was our last stop of the evening, so we didn't mind the wait.

I felt my phone buzz and saw that Tatum had responded to my email.

> *Evie,*
> *Another masterpiece! Would love to get the*
> *backstory to this piece. Can we talk tomorrow?*

I looked at Triniti and gave her an apologetic look as I respond to the Tatum's email.

> *Yes, tomorrow is great. I am free all day.*
> *Thanks.*

"Sorry about that. My agent"—*yes, I said agent.* I snickered to myself—"responded to me about my latest painting."

"Agent? Very nice. Did she like?" Triniti asked.

"I think so. She mentioned *masterpiece*, so I guess that's good."

As we advanced in line, we got to see the ice cream flavor menu. All the usual suspects were listed, but there was one that only an island ice cream store would serve—quahog.

I was next in line and ordered, "Butter pecan, one scoop in a cup."

Triniti, behind me, ordered the exact same thing. That just proved to me that we were meant to be friends.

We sat in the park and watched the people walk by as we ate our ice creams. Perfect island night. Just how I remembered them being when I'd been a kid. Ice cream had always made me feel better when I missed my mother, and butter pecan had been my grandparents' favorite flavor.

When we finished our ice creams, our bellies were full, so we decided to call it a night. Plus, I had to drive back up island. Triniti and I gave each other a wonderful hug and said our goodbyes. She promised to call before she left with the hopes that we could get together one more time.

The drive back up island was a quiet, uneventful trip. I always remembered having to be careful driving at night. The winding road had the ability, if not careful, to lull the driver to sleep. Deer were always a concern, especially at dusk when they were just coming out to eat, so I always tried to be alert.

I got home and grabbed my phone for my evening chat with Hendrix. Unfortunately, he was not available, and I was tired, so I left a messaging, saying I would call in the morning. I also sent a text to Reva, asking if she could come down this weekend, as I wanted to start cleaning out. She gave a quick response—a thumbs-up.

***

Tatum called the next day.

"Evie, hi."

"Hey, Tatum. So nice to hear your voice."

"Likewise. That is a pretty heavy painting you just completed. And the title, *Me*, must mean you are going through some stuff. I don't want to pry, but I like to give some backstory to all of the paintings I sell. It allows potential buyers to make a better connection."

"I understand," I told her then began giving more details on my move to the island and all of my new life discoveries.

"I always feel the emotions that you put into your paintings, but this one was overflowing with confusion and sadness, yet there was still focus and clarity. I don't know how you do it, but please keep it up. As I have said before, we are all better for it."

"Thank you."

"You are really starting to grow a following. I know that you haven't built your website yet, but I am being asked by a number of my buyers to be added to the notification list when you paint something new. Congratulations! This is how full-time artists build their business," she explained.

"Tatum, thank you for all of your help. You are the one helping to keep this dream of mine alive in this crazy journey."

"Always here to help. Keep me posted as you create more."

"Will do. And thank you."

***

For the remainder of the week, I sorted through things and started to separate what I would keep and what I would give away or sell. Reva was arriving on the two o-clock boat, so I left for the boat by one fifteen, wanting to make sure that I got a parking space so that I could meet her as she got off.

I did my usual focus on finding a great parking space and keeping myself calm so that I would not stress about how people were driving. I had to circle through town a couple of times before I found a spot, but the one I got was right next to the steamship authority. Amazingly, I had a few minutes, so I stopped and grabbed an iced coffee. Not like my normal Starbucks, but no matter. I had learned quickly to get over any of my fast food or franchise cravings, as there were no franchise chain restaurants on the island. Crazy but true. They were not allowed. However, there was one ice cream shop that slipped in, but no others had been allowed.

When the boat arrived, there was a stream of people, both walking and driving off. It looked like one of those clown cars that should only hold one person but fifty climbed out. I walked over to the boat, like so many others waiting for friends and loved ones at the bottom of the platform. I chose to stand in the back and saw Reva as she stepped through the door.

I jumped up and waved, yelling, "Reva!"

She gave me a nod in acknowledgement that she heard me. Then it took her a minute to get to me.

When we were finally close enough, she ran up, and we shared an enormous hug.

"Reva, it is *so* good to see you. How was the trip?"

"Hey, girl. Great to be seen." She pushed me back and looked me up and down. "What have you done to yourself? You look amazing. I guess island life has been treating you well."

"Ah, shucks," I goofed. "Thanks. Just a lot of sleeping, eating, and hard work."

"Nope. Nuh-uh, there is something else," she probed. "Have you met someone?"

My face turned a little red, and I laughed. "Maybe."

"Maybe, my ass. You met someone, and you didn't tell me," she accused.

"I wanted to tell you in person, and I didn't really know what it was until I got to the island."

"Well, I want to hear all about it."

I grabbed her bag, and we headed to the car. It didn't matter how long it took to drive up island, because we had a lot to catch up on.

When we pulled onto the road to my house, I swerved and jerked the car so that we would miss most of the bumps then looked at her and said, "Fixing this road is on my to-do list."

We got out, and I led the way to the house.

"Evie, this place is so cute, and the view is frigging awesome," Reva commented.

"Thanks. Yes, my grandparents were very proud of their little piece of paradise." I brought Reva's bag in and put it in my room. She followed me in.

"Apologies for the size of the bed. This is my old room. I haven't gotten to buying a new bed yet," I explained.

"Have you cleaned out your grandparents' room yet?"

"Nope, that is what I was hoping you could help me with. It's been an emotional rollercoaster so far, and I would prefer to do it with someone I trust."

"You know I am here for you. You have me for three full days. I have to be back in the City by Tuesday afternoon," she stated.

"Thanks."

We went back out to the living room, and Reva noticed my painting.

"I assume you painted this?"

"Yes, I did this after I opened the footlocker. As you can see, it was an emotional experience."

"It looks like it, but I do love the painting in a macabre way. New subject. I want to change the energy here. So, tell me about this special someone."

I proceeded to give Reva the details of how Hendrix and I had met, him helping me find my purpose and guiding me along my spiritual journey, and our first official date.

"Evie, you are just beaming. He must be something special. When do I get to meet him?"

"I don't know. He says that he will come and visit in August." I hesitated.

"I know you want him all to yourself," she observed. "No worries. When you are ready. So, where do we start?"

We started in my grandmother's closet. I had already cleaned out my grandfather's, but I had more sentimental attachment to Grandma's items.

The first night, we sorted through all my grandmother's clothes. I kept a few items, but most would be included in the estate sale or donated.

"Hey, Evie, did you see this?" Reva motioned me over.

"What?"

In the back of the closet were a number of canvasses. She carefully handed them out to me. In total, there were six paintings, all done by my grandmother. I had never seen these pieces before, and they weren't her usual landscape, detailed type paintings. She had used a technique called scumbling that gave the images unending depth and grandeur. We brought them out to the living room and leaned them up against the couch.

One painting was so extraordinary and familiar that I gasped when I saw it. I picked it up and turned it over. The title was *What I See When I Close My Eyes*. It was dated just a few years before she'd passed.

Reva watched me, knowing that this had made a huge impact on me. "Evie, what is it?

It took me a minute to answer. "This is exactly what *I* see when I close my eyes in meditation."

"What do you mean?"

"I see colors when I am in deep meditation, generally in the morning when I first wake up. These are the exact colors I see— violet, indigo, and green."

"If you are seeing colors like this in your meditation, then you are being shown your prominent chakras, or your prominent energy types."

"Holy shit, this is what Colbie meant by understanding my energy. She gave me a chakra book before I moved out here. I read through most of it but didn't understand how to apply it. So, my grandmother and I both had prominent Heart, Third Eye, and Crown chakras."

"Well, it seems like you and your grandmother were more connected than you thought."

My grandmother had been somewhat of a local celebrity artist, but she was known for detailed landscape paintings. These were vastly different. All of them dated between two to three years before she'd passed.

I looked over at Reva. "Do you think my grandmother had her awakening?"

"Or maybe she decided to paint what was really in her heart."

We sat in silence, just staring at the paintings. The silence was broken, however, by Mr. Brown's voice. I could hear him out in the yard.

"Evie, you there?" he called.

I went to the door and responded, "Yup, I'm here."

"Okay to come over? I got a surprise for you."

"Sure."

Mr. Brown walked in with a basketful of lobsters.

"What?" Reva yelled.

"Oh, sorry, I didn't know you had company."

"Mr. Brown, this is my best friend, Reva. She came up for a long weekend and to help me clean out and organize."

"Nice to meet you, Reva."

"It is wonderful to meet you, Mr. Brown, especially since you brought such a wonderful surprise," Reva said with a grin.

"Well then, ladies, I guess you have dinner tonight."

"Won't you join us?" I pleaded.

"I don't want to intrude. I'm sure you have a lot to catch up on," he added.

"Please, Mr. Brown. You bring us dinner, and then don't even join us? Unacceptable," Reva exclaimed, charming Mr. Brown into joining us.

The entire night, he told stories of me growing up—things that I never knew he knew. Reva ate it up, I'm sure for future blackmail. After Mr. Brown left, Reva and I leisurely cleaned the kitchen.

"Did you notice how Mr. Brown's face lit up when he talked about you?" Reva asked.

"No, I didn't, but he has been in my life since for as long as I can remember. Plus, he was my grandfather's best friend."

"Maybe, but that look was pride. He was genuinely proud of you."

"That's nice. He is a good family friend," I replied.

***

Later that night, I lay on the couch and gave my appreciation for the day to my higher self. Thinking back on the evening, it had been really nice to have Mr. Brown with me at this time. He had been my rock, and he had been so loving to me. I wondered how he knew those things. I was sure my grandparents had shared those stories with him.

In a whisper, I heard, *"Evie, enjoy your family."*

My family? I thought to myself. *What family?*

***

Over the next two days, Reva and I worked nonstop, sorting, cleaning, and organizing. My grandparents' bedroom was almost cleared out, except for my grandmother's jewelry and the footlocker, but I would let both of those wait.

Reva and I flopped ourselves onto the bed and stared at the ceiling.

"So, are you good sleeping in here now that everything is cleared out?"

"Yeah, I'm good," I mumbled.

"Whatever. What's up?"

"It's *their* room. I feel them in here."

"Do they scare you?"

"No, but it's still like I am intruding."

"Have you ever asked them to leave?"

"Why would I do that? It's their house."

"No, it is *your* house, and you can ask them to give you some time. Then, when you are ready, you can open yourself up to them again," Reva explained.

"I can do that?"

"Yes, you can. Evie, their energy is around you, all the time. They will always be with you. But, if you are not ready to hear them or feel them, you can request that they give you the time that you need. All they want to do is support you." She stood up. "I will leave you to it. I am going outside to sit on the deck. Come out when you are ready." With that, she closed the bedroom door.

I slipped off the bed and started pacing around the room. Then I heard, *"Speak from the heart."*

Nodding at the advice, I then took a deep breath and started. "Grandma and Grandpa, I miss you so much …" Tears started streaming down my face, and I paused to catch my breath. "Thank you for all that you did for me, to protect me and to raise me. I had no idea what you were all going through.

"You gave me a stable, loving life. But, as an adult, I was not able to create a joyful life. I have decided to change that, and coming back here is the start to my new, joyful life. I am here to paint and to create beauty, just like you taught me, Grandma.

"Learning about Mom has been very emotional for me. I understand why you all did what you did, but I cannot say that I have completely accepted it. Until I can do that and am ready to learn more, I ask that you give me the time that I need. I know you are always with me, but I need to make this my home, and I can't do that if I feel you in here. Please give me the time that I need. I love you."

I went into the bathroom and rinsed my face with cold water. Then I headed out to the deck where Reva was basking in the sun, looking extremely comfortable.

"Want to go to the beach?" I asked.

"You really needed to ask?"

We got ourselves together then drove over to the town beach. It was still a bit crowded, but we found a nice spot away from the families.

"So, how did it go?" she probed.

"I think it went well. I guess we will see when we get back."

We lay in the sun, in complete silence. After a few, I looked over at Reva. She was sound asleep.

***

After a few hours of basking in the sun, searching for wampum, and throwing each other in the water, we headed back home.

"I call first shower!" Reva yelled as she jumped out of the car.

I laughed, yelling after her, "Towels are in the bathroom closet."

I sat on the deck while she was in the outdoor shower. "Do you want to go downtown for dinner tonight and maybe find some trouble?" I shouted over the running water.

"Now you are talking," she shouted back.

I got in the shower after her, and then we got all gussied up. *Hmm ... I wonder where we should go?* Then I thought of Triniti. I gave her a call. Luckily, she picked up.

"Triniti, it's Evie."

"Hey, Evie. What's up?"

"I have a friend visiting, and we are heading down island tonight. Any recommendations? Plus, do you want to meet us?" I offered.

"Yes, I would love to! I am having dinner with some high school friends, then we could meet you for a drink. There are a few places I would recommend for dinner. There is the Ale House, Jake's Raw Bar, and the Dream Diner. We can meet you at Martha's for drinks. Say ... nine o'clock?"

"Perfect. Call if things change."

"Will do. See you tonight."

Reva and I were both feeling good. Nice glow from a day in the sun, summer dresses on, and we were actually going out to socialize. Hadn't done that in a while. I hoped I remembered how to make small talk.

We drove down island, windows down, music playing. It felt like we were back in college.

We pulled into town, and I did the usual parking space game. This time, we had two people focusing on a good spot, thus it manifested even quicker. It was a great spot, too—no time limit and in the middle of town.

We walked past the three restaurants that Triniti had suggested. Jakes and the Dream Diner all had lines, so we moved to the Ale House. Not too bad. Fifteen-minute wait, and we could get a seat on the deck. We went to the bar and ordered a couple of mojitos.

Reva noticed a couple of gentlemen at the end of the bar and gave me that look.

"No, not yet. Can't we just have dinner before you start?" I pleaded.

"Nope, you never know when you may meet Mr. Right."

"But I already have," I replied.

"Well, I haven't, and you are my wing girl, right?"

"Right," I responded with a sigh.

She gave the coy look then looked away, which signified *game on*. Next thing we know, our drinks are served with compliments from the two gentlemen. Reva nodded.

A few minutes later, we heard, "Good evening, ladies."

"Good evening, and thank you for your generosity. A good mojito can be hard to find," Reva stated.

"It was our pleasure. May we join you?"

"For a few, but we are just about to be seated for dinner," Reva responded.

Just like clockwork, we heard our names called to be seated.

"Thank you again, gentlemen, for your generosity. Have a nice evening."

"Hope to see you later," one of the men said as they went back to their seats at the bar.

"Reva, why did you do that? Now we are going to have to avoid them all night. This town is not that big," I scolded her.

"You may avoid, but the older one was cute." She laughed.

"Ugh."

We enjoy a wonderful dinner. Reva had surf and turf, and I had black cod—ethically sourced, of course—with a potato puree. Such an extravagant dinner. This place was unassuming but well worth the price.

I looked at my phone—eight forty-five—then told Reva that I was hoping to meet a friend from Colorado at another place around nine. Reva agreed.

We finished up and paid the bill. Before we left, though, I asked the bartender where Martha's was located, and he gave me directions.

Reva's new friends had overhead my question to the bartender, so I was sure we would be seeing them again tonight.

Walking down the main street was an event in itself. People were *everywhere*, sunburned and ready for whatever. However, we eventually found Martha's and strolled in.

I took a look around and saw Triniti at a table with three other women. I waved as we made our way over.

"Evie, you made it!" Triniti shouted over the loud music. She gave me a wonderful hug then introduced me to her friends. "Evie, this is Stacey, Trish, and Megan. We all went to high school together."

"Hello, everyone. And this is my friend, Reva."

Before we could get to the bar, a server brought us two mojitos.

We looked around and ... surprise-surprise, there was Reva's new friends.

Reva gave me a sideways look, as if to say, *don't screw this up for me.*

I smiled and did my duties as her wing girl. Luckily, by the time they made it to our table, I was deep in conversation with Triniti. It didn't seem to be a problem as the two gentlemen were happy to make conversation with Reva and the other women.

I looked at Reva to say, *you good?* and she gives me the okay wink.

Triniti turned to me and asked, "Are you settling in okay?"

"Yes. There have been a lot of emotions cleaning out my grandparents' house and learning things that I had no idea about, but overall, it really is starting to feel like home."

"Good. I know how it feels to start over. But, in the end, it is better to take that leap and completely rely on yourself than be miserable in a place that may be comfortable but is not healthy."

"So, how are you doing? You didn't mention much about your job and if it is going well when we went out to dinner."

"Yeah, the job is okay. It's just a job to pay the rent." She shrugged. "What I am really excited to do is sell my pottery. I make a few pieces here and there, but my goal is to get into a coop studio situation and sell my pottery regularly."

"With how positive you are, I am sure you will manifest exactly what you desire in no time. I love my piece."

"It is so nice to hear someone say that they believe in me. That is where my focus lies right now—in knowing *me*. My ex *thought* he knew me, and when I *strayed* from what he thought he knew, he would belittle me. At first, it was just little things, like *you don't know what you want*, then it escalated to him saying I was worthless. When you hear that enough, you start believing it. I lost all sense of who I was and wanted to become. Luckily, my friend saw what was happening and helped me get out. She was the one who helped me move the furniture. She is like you—pure light," Triniti explained.

"I am so happy to hear that you are doing well. Please let me know how I can help. My agent has a lot of connections, and I am sure she could advise on how to get your work out there."

The music steadily got louder, making it impossible for Triniti and I to continue our conversation. We headed back to the table, and I noticed Reva on the dance floor, having a ball. I told the others that I was going outside to make a phone call if Reva ended up looking for me.

I walked out of the bar, my ears still thumping. It took a few minutes for me to actually hear again as I sat on the curb, watching the people walk by and gave Hendrix a call.

"Hello," he answered.

"Hi, I miss you."

"Hey, you okay?

"Yes, I just miss you. Is it time for the passion hunter to take a vacation?"

"In another couple of weeks, I am sure I can make that happen."

"Good."

"Is everything okay? You sound a little down."

"I am out with Reva, and I just don't feel like I fit in anymore. It was nice talking to people one-on-one, but the whole party scene is just not comfortable. Plus, I was reminded how special you are, and I just wanted to let you know that I appreciate you," I shared.

"Wow, thank you, Evie. Now that you are on this journey, things that you used to find interesting may not be as interesting anymore. Just like people who you used to connect with, you may find that you have nothing to talk about with them anymore. It's all growing, making room for the things that are genuinely important to you."

"It feels kind of lonely at times," I confessed.

"It will, but you will find your people."

"You are my people," I gushed.

He chuckled. "Thank you. I love hearing that."

"Well, I better get back in there before Reva invites the entire bar back to my house. Thank you for being you."

Hendrix paused then asked, "Can I have a hug?"

I happily oblige.

"Thank you for that. I love feeling your energy. Have a good night."

Hanging up, I entered the bar and headed over to our table. Reva was in deep conversation with her new male friend. Triniti and her friends were laughing and telling stories with the other gentleman.

Reva looked at me and saw I had that *it's time to go* look. She excused herself from her friend and came over to me.

"You ready?" she asked.

"How did you know?"

"I know you," Reva replied. "Let me get his number, and then we can head out."

We said our good nights, and I gave Triniti a big hug and wished her well back in Colorado.

"Give a call anytime, and the offer still stands to talk to my agent," I promised before Reva and I zigged and zagged through the crowd to the door.

Outside, it was just as crowded in the streets as it had been in the bar. *Boy, summer is in full swing*, I thought to myself, needing to get out of the hubbub.

The drive up island was filled with Reva recounting her evening.

"His name is Brian, and he is an architect from Philly. Divorced, two kids, who are both out of college, and he is a foodie," she rambled on.

"Sounds like he is perfect for you."

"I thought so, as well. We exchanged numbers, and he said he would call me tomorrow on my trip back."

It hit me then like a ton of bricks. Reva was leaving tomorrow. I instantly became sad.

I could hear her rattling on about Brian, but it all seemed so far in the distance that I couldn't understand anything she was saying.

"Hey, Evie? Earth to Evie. What's up? You are you so quiet," she commented.

"Sorry, I forgot that you were leaving tomorrow. I have had so much fun with you being here that I don't want you to leave," I confessed.

"Evie, honey, I am only a phone call away, and it takes me no time to get back here. You know as well as I do that you still have some things to sort out, and it is best to do that in your time and on your own."

"I know, I know."

"Plus, isn't there someone special who is coming to visit soon? The man who I don't get to meet yet."

I blushed. "Yes, in a couple of weeks."

"Well, then I am sure that you will have plenty to do to get your house in order for your visitor."

We pulled onto the dirt road, bumping and swerving. In our haste to get down island, I had forgotten to turn on an outside light, so we climbed out of the car and fumbled our way to the front door.

"Evie, look up. Look at how bright the stars are tonight."

I smiled. "They are that bright every night."

In the distance, we could see the lighthouse's light—two reds and a white. It was a beautiful night.

We got ourselves ready for bed. I slept on the couch, promising Reva that it was just for one more night.

***

Traffic this morning was crazy. There must have been an accident or something, as we were not moving at all. My first chance, I took the back way into town. It was a little longer, but traffic the other way wasn't moving, so it was our best bet.

Luckily, Reva had purchased a roundtrip boat ticket, so our goodbye was quick, and it was basically a tuck and roll as I drove into the boat parking lot.

"Call me when you get back to the city," I yelled as she ran to the boat.

"Will do. I love you!"

"Love you, too. Thank you."

I slowly drove away, looking in my rearview mirror to make sure she made it on the boat.

She waved as she ran onto it.

CHAPTER 14 — FAMILY

The day was beautiful. I was out back, working in the garden, when I heard the ambulance coming up the main road. Growing up, my heart had always dropped when I heard that sound. Chances were you knew the person who needed the help.

The siren seemed to be getting closer, and then I realized that it was heading down Mr. Brown's road.

I dropped what I was doing and cut through the bushes to Mr. Brown's house. Just as I got there, the ambulance was pulling up. it seemed like the EMTs had already been there.

I ran up to one man and asked, "What's going on?"

"Sorry, but who are you?" he asked in return.

"I'm Mr. Brown's neighbor, Evie Prince."

"Oh, I heard you moved back. Nice to meet you. I'm Steve, volunteer fireman and EMT."

"Great, nice to meet you, but"—I gulped—"what's going on? Is Mr. Brown okay?"

"Attaquin should be fine. He called us because he was having chest pains. He wanted to be safe and asked to be brought to the hospital to be checked out. He is a tough one. I'm sure he'll be around for a long time to come," Steve asserted.

Just then, Mr. Brown was being rolled out of his house on a stretcher. I ran over to him.

"Hey, kid."

"*Hey kid?* What do you mean, *hey kid?* Are you all right? Why didn't you call me?" I bombarded him with questions.

"I didn't want to worry you. I'm okay, just want to get checked out."

As the EMTs wheeled him into the ambulance, he turned and asked, "Kid, can you do me a favor?"

"Of course. What is it?"

"I have a funny feeling they are going to want to keep me a few days since I'm old." He chuckled. "Can you grab me a set of fresh clothes and my PJs hanging on my bedroom door? I hate wearing those gowns that never close in the back."

"Will do, and I will bring them right down to the hospital."

"No rush. They will need to run lots of tests today, but if I could have them for tonight, that would be great."

Just before the EMTs closed the door, I waved to Mr. Brown, and he smiled.

The ambulance pulled out, and then the others followed behind. I was left in a cloud of dust.

A huge wave of emotion overcame me, and I started to cry. I kept on repeating, "He is going to be fine. He is going to be fine," as I climbed his stairs and opened the door. It felt like I had been in this house a thousand times, but now it felt so different.

I slowly walked down the hall, looking at everything with different eyes. Actually *seeing* everything, like pictures of him with what I believe is family. Funny, I never met any of his family. It always just seemed to be him. Then there were pictures of him on his boat, catching fish, and old pictures of him in his traditional regalia with others from his tribe.

I peeked into his bedroom, grabbed his PJs and bathrobe from behind the door, and then headed over to his dresser. I scanned the top for his brush and any other toiletry item he might need. I then looked up and saw myself in the mirror, noticing how worried I looked.

"He will be fine," I repeated.

Then I noticed a photo tucked into the corner of the mirror. It was a picture of my mother, a baby, and a man. I flipped the photo over and read the inscription.

Ava, Evie, and Paul. 1980.

I froze. Was this my father? How did Mr. Brown know my father?

I ran back down the hall and looked at his family photo. The same man was there.

My mind was in a swirl. I was confused.

I slid down the wall and just stared at the photo. Then I remembered what I had been told. *"Enjoy your family."*

Getting myself back together, I packed Mr. Brown's clothes and toiletries into a bag that I had found in his closet. I brought it over to my house, cleaned up, and got myself ready to head down to the hospital. Then I gave Hendrix a call before I left.

"Hello, Evie."

"Hi."

"What's up? You sound sad."

"Kind of. Mr. Brown was taken to the hospital with chest pains."

"Oh no. Is he okay?"

"He said he just wanted to be checked out. I'm just about to head down and bring him some items that he asked for."

"I am sure he will be fine. Just stay positive and send him some of your healing energy," he recommended.

"I also learned something else …"

"What?"

"Mr. Brown knew my father."

"How do you know?"

"There is a picture on his bedroom mirror … of my mother, me, and one of his family members … Paul."

"Whoa." He paused before asking, "How are you feeling?"

"Confused."

"Well, give yourself some grace. I am sure there is a lot more to learn."

"I will. I just want him to be okay."

"He will be. Take care of yourself and call me when you can."

"Will do."

I hung up then headed to the car, bag in hand.

In the middle of the driveway, I stopped and closed my eyes. I started to think about Mr. Brown and all the fun we had been having. My energy rose, and a smile crossed my face.

Universe, please give me light-filled healing energy.

My body filled with this energy that I felt build in my torso. Then I thought of Mr. Brown and focused my intention on sending this energy to him.

I send this light-filled healing energy to you, Mr. Brown, freely and openly, with love.

As the energy was sent, my torso relaxed, and I was left with peace.

***

The hospital seemed quiet. There weren't too many cars in the parking lot, either. I grabbed the bag and put on a fresh mask before heading to reception and asking for Mr. Brown's room. I was directed down the hall to room 111.

There, I knocked and heard, "Come on in."

"Mr. Brown, how are you doing?"

"Hey, kid. Thanks for bringing my stuff."

I nodded, but before I could say anything else, he said, "I'm okay. Been picked and prodded at for the last few hours."

"So, what's going on?"

"Oh, they think I have heart murmur. They don't know if I need surgery or just medication. Age is a buggar."

"Are you feeling okay? Are you in pain?"

"Nope. After I had the chest pain, things subsided. Don't worry, kid; I'll be okay," he said reassuringly.

"Would you like some company?"

"Please"

I sat, and he told me old fishing stories, and I let him know how the garden was progressing. They kicked me out just before

nine but said that family had extended hours and I could come
back tomorrow.

Family?

*Oh, Mr. Brown must have just said that so that I could visit
him*, I thought.

"I will see you again tomorrow, okay, Mr. Brown?"

"Evie, no need. I have all that I need. You don't have to
drive all the way down here just to hang out with an old man."

"Okay, that settles it. See you at nine tomorrow. Have a
great night." I closed his door, leaving him with a cheeky smile
on my face.

***

I arrived right at nine with a bag of pastries and a deck of
cards. I knocked, but he wasn't there.

I went to the nurses' station. "Excuse me. Where is Mr.
Brown? Is he okay?"

The nurse there smiled. "Yes, dear. He is still in testing, but
you can wait in his room, if you want."

"Thank you," I said with a ton of relief.

While I waited, I checked my phone. Cell service was still
better for me down island than up. I saw that I had missed an
email from Tatum.

> *Hi Evie,*
> *Hope you are well. Happy to tell you that
> your painting just sold for fifteen hundred over
> your original asking price. I had two interested
> parties, and the winner got it for four thousand
> five hundred. I will send the shipping information
> as soon as I confirm where he wants to receive it.*
> *Keep up the great work.*
> *Tatum.*

I look up from the phone with complete amazement. "I am
doing it!" I exclaimed.

Just then, the door opened, and Mr. Brown was rolled in, asking, "Doing what?"

"Hey, look at you. How do you feel?"

"Doing what?" he repeated.

"I am a full-time artist! I just got word that I sold another painting," I explained.

"Congratulations! I am so happy for you. I told you things would work out."

"Yes, you did," I replied with a grin on my face.

The nurse helped Mr. Brown into his bed.

"Thanks for bringing me my PJs and bathrobe. If I had just done that in one of those gowns, we all would have been in for a surprise."

The nurse blushed a bit, and we all laughed.

After the nurse left, I announced, "I brought you a surprise," and drop a bag of pastries in his lap.

"Is this legal?" He looked from side to side, as if there could be spies amongst us. "The food here is okay, but pastries are my favorite," he replied with a sheepish grin.

"I won't tell, if you don't. Plus, I also brought some cards. Figured we could play a little poker or something," I suggested.

"Poker. Now you're talking my language. You deal while I inhale one of these beauties." Mr. Brown held up a maple twist and, as promised, inhaled it.

We had a great time playing cards and gossiping about up-island life. Mr. Brown got all the latest from his visit to the dump the other day. I dealt us another hand.

"Mr. Brown, can I ask you a question?"

"Yeah, kid, what's up?"

"When I was in your house, I noticed a picture in the hallway of you and your family. How come I never met them? Do they not live here?"

"Oh, that picture. Yes, that was my older brother and sister. Both moved off island years ago. They both passed within the last ten years."

"I am sorry to hear that."

"They had a great life. It was just time for them to take a rest," he replied.

"Who was the young man also in the picture?" I probed.

"That was my son, Paul."

My heart skipped a beat as I gasp for air. "You said *was*. So, he died?" I asked gently.

"Yes, I lost him a few years ago. He was in the military and served in the Gulf War. He, unfortunately, was unable to adjust to civilian life and died of substance abuse," he lamented.

"Oh no. I am so sorry," I whispered.

"He wasn't happy here, in this physical life. Too many demons. I know he is in a better place. So … I guess, if you noticed the picture in the hallway, you also saw the picture on my bedroom mirror."

"Yes, I did." I dropped my head, embarrassed. "Was your son and my mother good friends?"

"They grew up together. So, yes, you could say that. Unbeknownst to me or your grandparents, they were more than childhood friends."

Mr. Brown looked at me then said what I knew in my heart to be true. "Evie, my son, Paul, was your father."

Stunned, I got up from my seat and paced the room. Not looking at him, not looking at anything.

From the other side of the room, I uttered, "And, why didn't anyone tell me?"

"Paul had demons even before he went into the military. He wanted to be a good father and be in your life, but he was unable to. He watched you from afar, and your mother kept him informed of how you were growing and your accomplishments. He just was incapable of being the man that he wanted to be as your father."

I felt like I was outside of myself. I must have looked pitiful—my head hung, my shoulders slumped. So many thoughts were going through my head. I didn't know what to do—walk out, or stay and ask more questions.

"Evie. Please know that he loved you so much. He was so proud of your accomplishments, and he was in awe that he was able to create such a beautiful human being. We all loved you and only wanted the best for you."

When I heard Mr. Brown say *we all loved you*, it was as if I had woken up from a crazy dream. Mr. Brown was my *grandfather*.

I walked to the side of his bed and stared at his weather-worn, brown face. I noticed his eyes filling with tears.

He grabbed my hand and squeezed it. "You have been my pride and joy. I love you, kid."

I broke down, sobbing, kneeling by his bed and putting my head on his hand. There was nothing that I could say. I just rested there until my last tear was shed. Finally, I looked at him and noticed how lovingly he was looking at me.

"Are you okay with me being your grandfather?" he asked.

I stood, holding his hand, and said, "Now you're talking my language."

***

Bright and early, I was back at the hospital, waiting to bring Mr. Brown—my grandfather—back home.

"Good morning. You ready to go home?" I asked as I peeked into his room.

"Yup, let's blow this popsicle stand," he replied with a smile.

I grabbed his bag, and then we headed out the door.

He handed me some papers as we walked out—discharge orders and prescriptions. "Need to fill these before we get back up island," he states.

"No problem. I suppose we need to pick you up some food, as well. Do you feel up for it, or should I take you home first?"

"Don't worry about me. I can sit in the car, if you don't mind. I don't want to have to deal with summer folk just yet."

"Understood. Let's go to the pharmacy first, and then you can make your list of what I need to get."

We finished our errands then headed up island.

Once we got out of the mess of downtown, Mr. Brown—Granddad—let out a big breath of air.

"You okay?" I asked, looking worriedly over at him.

"Yup, just letting go of all that noise from down island. I don't like bringing that type of energy back home with me."

I nod in agreement. "You speak of energy often. Have you always lived your life this way?"

Granddad thought for a moment then replied, "When I was younger and was learning the spiritual ways from my elders, I was very aware and focused on energy. As I got older, however, I didn't pay as much attention. My ego took the reins, and my life was not what I wanted it to be. I did what was expected and, in the end, I was not happy. It took a string of events to wake me up and help me remember what life is all about. From that point on, I have been very aware of my and others' energy. Energy is everything, and when you remember that, life is so much more enjoyable."

"Do you speak to others about energy?" I probed.

"Not really. It is just how I choose to live my life. If others are aware and focus on their energy, as well, I am happy to engage. For those who are unaware, or just think this is some kind of hocus pocus or Native American medicine man kind of thing, I don't feel it is necessary to engage. They won't hear, anyway," he explained.

"Thanks. I am still trying to figure this whole thing out. Seems like I am meeting more and more people who are aware, but I still don't feel comfortable being so open with them."

"Don't worry; you just do what makes you comfortable."

We arrived back at the house before lunch. I brought Granddad in and made him comfortable before grabbing the stuff from the car.

"You know, I am not going to break," he yelled as I went back outside.

"I know, but I don't want you doing too much too soon," I said when I came back in, carrying his bag to his room then unpacking the groceries.

"What would you like for lunch?

"Tuna sandwich," he replied.

"Coming right up." I made the sandwich then set him up on the couch.

He looked over at me. "Aren't you going to have something?"

"No, I am good. I just want to make sure you eat. What time do you want dinner? I'll come back over to make you something?"

"I like to eat at five."

"Got it. I will be back before then to make dinner. Gotta go now. I have a guest coming to visit, and I still need to clear some things out," I explained.

"Anyone I know?" he asked jokingly, knowing full well that he wouldn't know the person.

"No, he is a friend of mine from Colorado."

"He, huh?"

"Yes, he."

"Okay, better get to it. See you tonight."

***

For the next few days, I cooked my grandfather three square meals and made sure he took his medicine. By the fourth day, he kicked me out.

"Okay, kid, it's been nice having you around, but I am good now. I need to get up and start doing this on my own. Plus, I am fixing to go fishing this afternoon."

"Fishing?" I exclaimed.

"Yes, fishing. I will take my medicine before I head out. Don't worry about me."

"You know I do," I responded.

He smiled. "Yes, I know you do. Now get out and live your life."

For the next week or so, I cleaned out more stuff, unpacked more boxes, went to the dump, and worked in the garden. When all was said and done, I really felt like I had made this my home. There was one glaring anomaly, though—my grandparents' bedroom. That was for later.

CHAPTER 15 — SOMEONE SPECIAL

"I can't believe I will actually see you tomorrow," I squealed.

"It has been too long," Hendrix replied.

"I will be waiting at the airport. Please travel safe, and I will see you tomorrow."

"Will do. Can't wait to see you. Big hug."

I felt his energy as if he was standing in front of me, hugging me himself.

"Mmm ... I love how you do that."

Later, I could barely sleep. I went into every room to make sure that the house looked perfect.

I knew that I had promised Reva that I would move into my grandparents' room, but I still hadn't. So, I changed the sheets on the bed in my room since I didn't know what the actual sleeping arrangements would be, grabbed a blanket, and slept on the couch.

at two o'clock in the afternoon, I was on the road, heading down to the island airport. I had never flown into the island before, so I was not familiar with the airport and wanted to get there early. Traffic wasn't bad, and I had no problem finding parking.

The airport was really nice. Cute, just like you would see in that 1990's TV show, *Wings*. Cedar shakes and white trim.

I slipped into the waiting area and checked the board for his arrival time. Great, he was on time. I went to the snack shop to grab a cold drink then took a seat. Looking over to my left, I notice that an older couple were watching me. When I caught their eye, they both smiled

The woman asked, "Waiting for someone special?"

Red-cheeked, I responded, "How did you know?"

"Telltale signs—constantly looking at your reflection, fixing your hair, trying to sit quietly but you repeatedly look at the arrival board. I have seen it all before and have done it before." She laughed.

Just as I was about to respond, the announcement that flight 482 from Boston had just landed came over the speaker.

I jumped up and fixed myself one last time. Then I looked over at the couple, who I hadn't noticed before were holding hands.

They both smiled, and she said, "Enjoy every moment and have a wonderful time."

Standing there, I could feel a huge surge of energy running through me. It almost took my breath away. At the exact same moment, Hendrix walked through the gate.

With a big, beautiful smile, he dropped his bags and embraced me like I had never felt before. The energy flowing between the two of us was visible. The world stopped, and everything went quiet.

When I eventually opened my eyes and loosened my embrace, I noticed we were in the middle of all the people exiting the plane, but they just walked around us.

I looked up at Hendrix with a big, cheesy smile and said, "Hi."

"Hi. So nice to see you," he responded.

Our eyes never left each other. We just stared as if we were memorizing each other's face. Finally, we both laughed.

I went to grab one of his bags at the exact moment that he bent down to pick them up and ... *wham!* we bumped heads.

"Ouch," I whimpered.

"You okay?" he asked then leaned over and kissed my forehead to make it all better. It was so awkward and clumsy but romantic all at the same time.

As we exited the airport, I noticed the couple watching us. Both had these wonderful smiles on their face, as if they were watching themselves at some point in time in their own lives.

I smiled at them and said, "Have a great day."

When we got in the car, I felt so nervous. At first, I didn't know what to do or say. It was like I had forgotten how to drive.

Hendrix placed his hand on my arm, and I took a deep breath, resetting everything. Now I was ready.

"How was the flight? Was it scary being on a puddle jumper?"

"It was definitely interesting. They asked my weight before I boarded the plane, and I didn't get to pick my seat. They told me where to sit so that the weight on the plane would be evenly distributed. Once we were up, it seemed like we were already coming down. But the view was absolutely breathtaking. Such an experience."

"I have never flown to or from the island. I guess I will need to add that to my bucket list."

As I drove, I could feel Hendrix looking at me. It was such an incredible feeling having him here with me. I had originally planned on being tour guide, but I thought better of it, as it was a long trip and he must be tired.

We pulled onto the dirt road, and I did the normal driving dance to avoid the bumps and holes. Under my breath, I said, "One day, I will fix this road."

I parked the car then popped the trunk as Hendrix climbed out and looked at the house.

"Evie, this is a beautiful house. Such a breathtaking location."

"Thank you. It really has become my sanctuary."

I helped Hendrix carry his bags into the house, and we placed them in my old room. Then I gave him the tour. We ended up on the back deck, looking at the lighthouse. Two red and one white.

"The lighthouse is mesmerizing. I could watch this all night."

"That's what I used to do when I lived here with my grandparents and missed my mother. I just stared at the lighthouse, and it calmed me."

It was wonderful having Hendrix with me. We made a simple dinner of grilled fish, courtesy of my granddad, with a salad and wild rice. Hendrix and I gave each other space, but there was a force that kept drawing us closer, just like at the airport. I would reach for the salad dressing at the same time he would, our fingers gently touching.

"Who knew you were such a great chef," Hendrix commented

"Please, it's nothing. It's not as easy just to run out and grab something to eat here. To survive, you have to learn to cook. Plus, Mr. Brown always keeps me stocked with fresh fish."

"I look forward to meeting this Mr. Brown. He has really become an important part of your life," he noted.

"More than you know," I said with a smile on my face.

We went out on the deck and enjoyed a nice glass of wine. Hendrix sat on the couch, and I sat on the chair next to him.

"Evie, I can't tell you how nice it is to just sit here with you. I really have missed your energy."

"I feel the same way. I don't remember ever feeling so peaceful."

As the sun set, the temperature got cooler. I shivered.

"Do you want to go inside?" he asked.

"No, let me just grab a blanket," I replied.

When I returned, Hendrick slid over on the couch. "If you are cold, you can join me, and I can keep you warm."

I blushed as I sat down next to him.

"Don't worry; I won't bite. Lean back and relax."

I did so, feeling his chest rise and fall with each breath. It felt so good to actually have him next to me.

"I didn't know the stars could be so bright," he whispered.

I was in heaven. My body just fit perfectly in his side. His chest rocking me into a peaceful trance, and his strong arm wrapped around me, warming my body. Pure heaven.

Next thing I knew, Hendrix was whispering in my ear, "Evie, wake up. It's time to go inside."

"Huh? Oh, sorry. I must have fallen asleep," I replied.

"We both fell asleep. Let's go to bed."

Ooo ... hearing him say *let's go to bed* sounded so good to my ears. But wait—which bed? We hadn't even kissed yet. I didn't want to assume.

My body stiffened as I sat up.

"Are you okay?" he asked.

"Yes, I'm fine. Let me get your room ready," I replied quickly, scurrying into the house.

Hendrix came in a few minutes later and set the wine glasses in the sink. He then walked into the room, asking, "Evie, what's the matter? Are you okay?"

"I'm sorry. I just got nervous." I turned my back to him and explained, "I don't know what to do."

"What do you mean, *what to do*?"

"We haven't even kissed yet, and I don't know where you should sleep or where you want to sleep," I babbled, barely making any sense.

Hendrix put his hands on my shoulders and turned me around. He looked me straight in the face, and I looked into his deep brown, loving eyes. He then pulled me in for one of his amazing hugs. My body completely relaxed.

"Evie, stop worrying. There is no pressure. Whatever makes you comfortable."

"You make me comfortable," I told him, looking up at him.

He then bent down and gave me the most delicious kiss that I had ever experienced. His lips were so soft ...

I melted into him and enjoyed the wonderous moment.

When we separated, I thought we were both shocked at how extraordinary the kiss had been. I tried to pull myself together, but we were both flabbergasted.

"I made this bed for you. I am sorry it is so small. I haven't had time to buy something bigger."

"This is perfect."

I turned to walk out of the room, but before closing the door, I looked back at him, so wanting to join him, but I resisted and gently closed the door.

I set myself up on the couch, and just as I was settling in, I heard the bedroom door open. Hendrix went into the bathroom, and I slumped down so that he wouldn't see me. I didn't want to have to explain why I was sleeping on the couch.

As he turned to go back into his room, I felt his eyes come over to the couch.

"Evie, why are you sleeping on the couch? I thought you had moved into the other room by now."

I sheepishly answered, "I had hoped to, but I still can't bring myself to sleep in there."

He walked over to me and took my hand before leading me into my room and laying me down on the bed. He then pulled the covers over me and lay down on top of the covers next to me. I could feel his warm body next to mine.

"Sleep, Evie, sleep," was the last thing that I remembered hearing.

***

"Good morning, beautiful"

Just as I wake up, I smell coffee. *Mmm ... I love the smell of coffee.* I slowly opened my eyes and saw him, Hendrix, standing there in just a pair of shorts. He had an amazing body and a beautiful smile, holding a cup of coffee. I must have died and gone to heaven.

A broad smile crossed my face. "Good morning. How did you sleep?"

"Like a baby. And you?"

"That was the most sound sleep I have had since being in this house. Mmm … you made coffee. Thank you."

He handed me the cup and sat on the bed, just gazing into my eyes.

At first, I was a little shy. Who knew what I looked like? But his face was so sincere that I could not help but fall deep into his gaze.

"You really are perfect," he whispered.

I looked down and blushed.

He then leaned over and gave me a sweet kiss on the forehead.

"So, what would you like for breakfast?"

"You're making breakfast?"

"Sure. Why not? You made dinner. I make a mean French toast."

"That sounds delicious."

I crawled out of bed and moved to sit at the kitchen table while Hendrix made his mean French toast. For such a big man, he was so fluid in his movements. He definitely knew his way around a kitchen, too.

"The coffee is so good! Did you put something in it?" I probed.

"Maybe … You will have to get up awfully early to get that secret from me." He turned around, holding two plates stacked high with mouthwatering French toast.

"Yum, this looks so good. Thank you."

"My pleasure." He smiled. "Oh, I met your neighbor, Mr. Brown. He was a very pleasant man."

"You did? How did that happen?"

"I was out on the deck, meditating and enjoying the sunrise, when I heard some funny noises, as if someone was trying to lift something. I poked my head through the bushes and asked if he needed help. Honestly, he was a bit surprised, but I introduced myself and gave him a hand. I also thanked him for taking such wonderful care of you. His response was interesting. He said, *that's what families do.* I just nodded and returned back to the house."

"Yes, that is what families do," I repeated.

"Okay, there is something going on here. Can I have a clue?"

I laughed and stuffed another bite of French toast into my mouth. After I finish chewing, I explain all that had happened over the past few weeks—Mr. Brown going into the hospital, me seeing pictures of my mother and father, and learning that Mr. Brown was, actually, my grandfather.

"What? Your grandfather?" he said in pure shock. "Your whole life, you had no idea?"

"Nope. He was always around, but I thought it was because he was my grandfather's best friend."

"That is such an amazing surprise."

"It was."

"How do you feel about it?"

"Initially, I was in shock, but then that shock turned to pure joy. He has always been special to me. He knew how to talk to me when I was growing up and confused. Was there when I got into trouble. Explained life to me. He just always knew when something was up."

"And your grandparents didn't tell you because …?"

"It seems that neither my mother nor my father were parent material, so they just thought it best that my grandparents raise me after my mother's death so that I would not be influenced by my parents' choices or lifestyles. It does make me sad that I missed so much time with Mr. Brown," I lamented.

"You can't change the past, so don't dwell there. Stay present and enjoy the time that you have with him now," Hendrix encouraged.

We finished breakfast then moved out to the deck to enjoy the early sun before it got too hot.

***

Day by day, Hendrix and I grew closer and closer. We explored the island, went swimming, meditated on the beach, and just enjoyed each other's energy. Each night, we were innovative and slept anywhere but my grandparents' room. Tonight, we slept under the stars.

I had designed a makeshift bed out of cushions, pillows, and blankets to soften the hard deck. It was like we were eight years old, camping out. I nuzzled into the crook of Hendrix's arm as we looked up at the stars.

"Hendrix, thank you for being so understanding."

"What? I love camping," he said with a smile.

"I know this is something that I have to get over, but I don't know what is holding me back."

"Did you ask?"

"Did I ask what?" I replied

"Did you ask your higher self what is holding you back?"

"No, I didn't think to do that."

"Maybe that is something that you should focus on. Ask, and you will be answered," he reminded me.

I rolled over and looked deeply into his eyes. Caressing his face, I asked, "How did I get so lucky to have you in my life?"

"You know it is not luck," was his reply.

"Yes, but I don't remember asking specifically for you."

"Manifestation works in funny ways. You may not have asked specifically for me, but there were qualities in me that you desired. Thinking of me raised your energy, and your desire to see me made it come into being. Just like how I thought of you.

"I had thought about you since we first met, but I was not ready, and it didn't seem like you were either. When we got reacquainted, I desired having the opportunity to be with you. Every time I thought about your beauty, creativity, and energy, *my* energy would soar. This was meant to be, and we made it happen. We created this experience."

I reached up and kissed him gently. The energy that I felt when he had first arrived at the airport was nothing compared to what was happening now. My whole body was electrified. His energy matched mine.

We kissed and gently explored each other's bodies. This was nothing like I had ever experienced. Pure magic. There was no urgency. He was passionate, gracious, and loving. When our bodies finally came together, the energy was magnificent, flowing between the two of us on this endless loop of electricity and ecstasy. The beauty of it all was overwhelming and, when it ended, I cried.

"Evie, is everything okay?"

"Yes." I giggled. "It was wonderful. That was the most amazing experience I have ever had in my life. Thank you," I sighed out.

"No, thank you. I have been waiting for this moment for so long. I knew it would be glorious. It was everything that I knew it could be and more. I love you, Evie Prince."

I had longed to hear those words, and now it had happened. Someone loved me for me. In all my quirkiness, someone loved me.

In my head, I was screaming, *I love you, too, Hendrix Talisman*, but the words would not come out of my mouth. I looked at him and said, "I ..." Then I looked away.

***

Early the next morning, I gazed at Hendrix's sleeping face and thought, *Did that really happen?* I glowed, thinking back on the evening.

Yes, it really did happen.

I slipped out from under his arm and snuck away to meditate.

Green and purple colors flowed in and out of my vision, creating a delicate dance between the two. Then the colors disappeared, and I saw brightness and heard, *"Forgive them, and you will be free."*

***

Our last two days together, Hendrix and I were physically inseparable. As clever as we were sleeping in different locations, we were equally as clever in where we made love. Each time, I fell more and more in love with him. Yes, he was handsome, had an amazing body, and knew exactly what I liked, but it was his spirit and energy that captivated me. He was part of me physically and spiritually. Hendrix and I became one.

The drive to the airport was quiet. I didn't know how I was going to manage not having him with me, and I was freaking out because I didn't know when I would see him again.

I could feel him looking at me.

"Evie, don't be sad," he pleaded. "We will see each other again soon. We will make it happen."

"I know, but …" I trailed off.

"We both have things we have to work on. These are things that we must do on our own. When we are ready, we will see each other again, and I believe, when that happens, it will be for good."

"For good?" I asked, not really understanding what he meant.

"Yes, Evie. I know we will be together. It just may take a little longer till it happens. When it gets hard, remember our energy and love for each other. You can only love someone else when you truly love yourself."

We pulled into the airport, and I parked the car. Then he grabbed his bags, and we walked to security. His flight was on time. My eyes started to well up.

He looked at me, bent down, and kissed me firmly but gently on the lips. Then he enveloped me in one of his warm, loving hugs and whispered, "Remember, I love you, Evie Prince."

No matter how much I wanted to tell him that I loved him, I couldn't reply.

Through my tears, I watched as he walked away. When I could no longer see him, I turned and ran to the car. I felt like I was disappearing. I felt nothing. I was in a fog.

I arrived home but don't remember how I got there. Walking into the house, I stumbled from room to room, not knowing what to do or where to go. I walked into my room and saw something on the bed. Hendrix's T-shirt. I gently picked it up and held it to me, breathing in his scent. Then I curled up on the bed, hugging his shirt, and fell into a deep sleep.

***

"Evie, you home?" I heard my granddad call. "Evie?"

"I'm here," I replied weakly, rising from the bed then making my way to the kitchen.

"Hey, kid." Granddad bounded into the kitchen, all smiles. Then he looked at me and stopped dead in his tracks. "You okay, kid? What's wrong?"

"I'm okay." I paused. "Hendrix left today."

"Oh. When does he plan on coming back?"

"He said we both have to work on things, which is true. So, there is no definite date, but when he does, he believes it will be for good."

"Well, that sounds pretty serious. I guess you like him then."

"You could say that," I replied with a smile.

"Did he tell you that I met him?"

"Yes, he did. He also said that he almost gave you a heart attack."

"You got that right. Who in their right mind slips through the bushes that early in the morning and casually asks if I need help? Granted, I did need help, but I wasn't expecting a six-foot-three, muscular black man to be the one offering it. You love him?"

"I'm afraid to."

"I get it, kid. I used to be the same way. But I found out that it's not really fear. You just don't feel worthy of love. It took me a while to work through all that, and it is still a work in progress. But, once I figured out why I had those thoughts and learned to love myself, the relationships that I have now are healthier and more fulfilling. Knowing that you are worthy changes the game. You understand what you want and you stop settling. In the end, it is only you, so it's best to figure out how to love yourself, because no one else's love will matter until you do." He stopped and gave me a warm, caring smile.

"Oh, I almost forgot. I brought you something." He handed me a bag of steamers. "Thought you may want some for dinner tonight."

"Ooo ... Thank you."

He grabbed my hand and gave it a squeeze. Then, as he turned to walk out, he said, "Remember, kid, you are loved. Now you just have to figure out how to love yourself."

***

The rest of the week, I woke thinking that Hendrix would be lying in bed with me. And, each morning, I found myself disappointed. A wave of sadness came over me, and then I would reminisce about the time we had together, and my energy rose. I forced myself to go into my grandparents' room to think about how I would like it to be, then I would turn around and retreat to the living room.

Today, I was feeling especially sad. I needed to talk with Hendrix.

"Good morning, sweetheart," he crooned.

"Good morning. Needed to hear your voice this morning. How was your night?"

"For some reason, I am unable to sleep in a bed. I am so used to sleeping on couches and decks that I am not comfortable in a normal, queen-sized bed anymore," he teased.

"Ha-ha, very funny. It's location and not the company?" I retorted.

"Okay, you caught me. I don't like sleeping without you next to me."

"I don't like it, either."

"It won't be too long. I want to give you the best of me, and I am working to make that happen."

"I understand, and I am working on my issues, as well, but I still don't like that you are so far away."

"I know." I paused then said, "Hey, I have to go, but I will call you again tonight. I love you, Evie Prince."

"I … I will talk to you tonight."

After we hung up, I heard, *"Paint, Evie, paint."*

"What should I paint?" I asked.

"Paint your feelings."

I grabbed my stuff and set up the easel on the back deck, like my grandmother used to always do. Closing my eyes, I immediately saw color. Green and red pulsated back and forth. Then I landed on red. Root chakra. The emotions flowing through me ranged from anger to love, fear to courage, resentment to understanding. I opened my eyes and began to paint.

Long, sweeping strokes were interrupted by heavy smears and brush stabs. Red, purples, and pinks were the primary colors. Everything was twisted like vines, dependent on each other but also trying to break free. The outcome emphasized a perpetual struggle.

I stepped back and looked at the finished piece. Beauty and anger resonated off the canvas. I leaned against the railing, completely depleted. Before my eyes, I could see my internal struggle.

"I need to heal … I want to heal!" I screamed.

Then a calmness overtook me, and I heard, *"Forgive, and you will heal."*

***

The relationship dream returned to me tonight. I saw myself from behind, walking on the beach, holding hands with a man. I heard a child's voice in the distance say, "Daddy! Wait up!" Then the man turned to me and smiled.

The words, *"You are ready,"* startled me out of my dream, and I sat up, looking around.

I slipped out of bed and went directly to the kitchen to grab the key from the windowsill. Closing my eyes, I put my hand on my heart center and declared, "I will heal." Then I went to the footlocker, slowly put the key into the lock, and turned …

To Be Continued...

ABOUT THE AUTHOR

Inspirational writer, Victoria Wright has embarked on a journey to find her true self. In the process, she is remembering how to be whole, to look inward for guidance, and to know her truth. Her journey is full of beauty and discovery. She invites you to join her on your own journey of remembering.

To learn more about Victoria and her work visit: www.HealingWords.online.

www.ingramcontent.com/pod-product-compliance
Lightning Source LLC
Chambersburg PA
CBHW050135110726
47898CB00008B/2540